631688

Ferr   Ferrars, E   X
        Drowned rat
5.95

DATE DUE			

DEPARTMENT OF LIBRARY AND ARCHIVES
Box 537
Frankfort, Kentucky 40601

Drowned Rat

By E. X. Ferrars

DROWNED RAT
HANGED MAN'S HOUSE
THE SMALL WORLD OF
   MURDER
FOOT IN THE GRAVE
BREATH OF SUSPICION
A STRANGER AND AFRAID
SEVEN SLEEPERS
SKELETON STAFF
THE SWAYING PILLARS
ZERO AT THE BONE
THE DECAYED GENTLEWOMAN
THE DOUBLY DEAD
THE WANDERING WIDOWS
SEEING DOUBLE
SLEEPING DOGS
FEAR THE LIGHT

DEPART THIS LIFE
COUNT THE COST
KILL OR CURE
WE HAVEN'T SEEN HER
   LATELY
ENOUGH TO KILL A HORSE
ALIBI FOR A WITCH
THE CLOCK THAT WOULDN'T
   STOP
HUNT THE TORTOISE
THE MARCH MURDERS
CHEAT THE HANGMAN
I, SAID THE FLY
NECK IN A NOOSE
THE SHAPE OF A STAIN
MURDER OF A SUICIDE
REHEARSALS FOR A MURDER

Drowned Rat

E. X. FERRARS

PUBLISHED FOR THE CRIME CLUB BY

DOUBLEDAY & COMPANY, INC.

GARDEN CITY, NEW YORK

1975

All of the characters in this book
are fictitious, and any resemblance
to actual persons, living or dead,
is purely coincidental.

Library of Congress Cataloging in Publication Data

Ferrars, E. X.
Drowned rat
I. Title.
PZ3.B81742Dr3 [PR6003.R458] 823'.9'12
ISBN 0-385-07292-9
Library of Congress Catalog Card Number 74-33640

Copyright © 1975 by M. D. Brown
All Rights Reserved
Printed in the United States of America
First Edition in the United States of America

CHAPTER ONE

It happened so fast, the cry, the splash, the flailing of strong arms across the still water to what lay sprawled at the bottom of the pool under the shade of the chestnuts that Catherine Gifford afterwards was never certain that she answered as truthfully as she might the questions that were to be put to her later. Had she or had she not seen anyone among the trees?

Her thoughts had been far away at the time. She and Andie Manson had been strolling up the path from her home towards Havershaw, the house that for a year had belonged to Douglas Cable. They had been invited there for drinks. Andie had come to call for her half an hour earlier, bringing her a present, one of his small wood carvings, which she happened to like rather better than she liked most of his work. She had never told him so, but a great deal of what he did meant nothing to her. But Douglas Cable had said it was outstanding, and from the skill with which he had refurnished Havershaw, it could be assumed that he knew what he was talking about. However, the thin, spiky, restless shapes that Andie loved generally had very little appeal for Catherine, who had found recently, she could not have said why, that she liked things solid, firm and understandable.

She had been brooding as they walked along. The fact that today's present had some of the qualities that she liked did not help her at all to make up her mind how to say to Andie what she thought she must. She had been almost silent as they walked along the path, the short cut across Douglas's fields from her home to Havershaw. Andie had been silent too, but then he was never much of a talker until he had had two or three drinks. Once he had had them, he could talk all too much and be quarrelsome too, but this evening he was reticent, self-absorbed and quite sober.

Then all of a sudden he had given a yell, taken three strides, gone in a long, shallow dive into the new swimming pool and was swimming across it before Catherine had even seen the object at the far end, just below the diving board.

Even then for an instant she did not recognise it. She saw spread-eagled limbs, made greenish by the reflection in the water of the trees grouped about the pool. Limp, helpless limbs, naked except for short red swimming trunks. She saw brown hair that looked soft and wavy like weed floating around the hanging head. Then, without knowing what it was about the body that had told her so, she knew that it was Douglas.

By that time she was halfway round the pool, running towards the steps to which Andie was hauling the body and where he would need help to drag it out. She caught at Douglas under the arms as Andie thrust him upwards. She felt wet arms slither round her neck and Douglas's head loll on her shoulder. But his weight was far too great for her strength and she felt the head and arms begin to slide away from her, back into the water.

Andie shouted at her, "Hold on!" and gave a heave to the long legs, managing to lift one of them over the edge of the pool on to the paving round it.

Head and arms and torso were wet and slippery. Clinging to them felt like fighting the unconscious man in a clammy, eerie battle. Then Andie pushed Douglas's second leg up beside the other, climbed out of the pool and dragged him further from the edge.

With a sharp shudder of relief, Catherine disengaged herself from the deathlike hold that Douglas had had upon her and stood up. Wet patches blotched the cream-coloured silk dress that she was wearing. Her copper-red hair, curving sleekly up from her shoulders a few moments before, was splashed and ruffled. Her clear, very fair skin looked whiter than usual. But her grey eyes were calm. She was a doctor's daughter and for her age had had considerable experience of what pain and the fear of death could do to others.

"Is he dead?" she asked softly.

"Not yet," Andie said. He was feeling for the beating of the heart and gave a little hiss of satisfaction as he found it pulsing. "This is where one gives the kiss of life, I believe. I've never done it, though I was once shown how and I'll have a try at it. If I finish the poor bloke off it'll be just too bad. You'd better get to a telephone as fast as you can and call an ambulance."

His breathing was short and harsh. He hardly ever sounded as Australian as he did just then.

His black hair hung in wet streaks over his long, narrow, bronzed face and into the eyes that looked so startlingly blue against the tanned skin. His soaked clothing, a black shirt and light blue cotton trousers, clung to his long, thin body. As Catherine left, running, he straightened out the limbs of the unconscious man and stooped over him.

Havershaw was nearer than Catherine's home so she went straight on towards it. She caught herself thinking that Irene was not going to like this. She was not going to like having her plans for her little party upset. Her plans were always carefully, rather reluctantly made, but once she was committed to carrying them out she hated any interference with them. She was not a callous woman. A matter of life and death would not seem unimportant to her. But she would probably be alarmed in a peculiar way at not being able to stick to the ritual that she had worked out for the evening.

The big house was out of sight from the pool, hidden from it by the screen of chestnuts. It was only after Catherine had emerged from the trees on to the lawn beyond that the house appeared, a square Georgian building, dignified and comfortable, built of rosy brick that seemed to hold the warmth of the evening sunshine. A paved terrace ran along the length of it, edged with tufts of rock roses, brought into full bloom, after the damp and chill of the early summer, by the sunshine of the last few days. The lawn sloped up to the edge of the terrace. Catherine crossed it, plunged straight in at the open glass doors that led into a small, pretty sitting room, went on through it into the long passage beyond, and called, "Irene! Elspeth! Is anybody there?"

A door opened immediately and a servant appeared. Catherine did not think that she had ever seen her before. Keeping servants was not one of Douglas's talents. Or perhaps the fault was Irene's. All the old faces that had been there for years in the time of old Mrs. Cable, Douglas's aunt, had vanished. This was a middle-aged woman in a neat nylon overall.

"I think Mrs. Cable's changing," she said. "And Miss Wilde too. They just came in from having a swim. It's such a lovely day, isn't it? Will you wait in the sitting room, or perhaps you'd sooner sit on the terrace? I'm sure they won't be more than a few minutes."

"Please, I've got to telephone," Catherine said. "There's

been an accident down at the pool. Mr. Cable must have hit his head on something. He's half drowned. Mr. Manson's looking after him, but we've got to get an ambulance as fast as we can."

The woman gave a little cry of shock and took Catherine back into the sitting room, through which she had just come, where there was a telephone on a small piecrust table.

"I'll tell Mrs. Cable at once," the woman said. "Who shall I say brought the message?"

"Miss Gifford." Catherine picked up the telephone and began to dial 999. "She was expecting me for drinks anyhow—" She broke off to speak to the exchange to ask to be put in touch with the ambulance service.

While she spoke to the voice that answered, the woman in the overall went quietly out and only a minute or two later Irene Cable darted into the room, reaching for the zip of her floating, flowery dress, trying to straighten it on her hips and to smooth back her short black hair.

She was a tall, bony woman of forty-five whose joints looked too loosely fitted together for her to be able to move competently and purposefully in any direction, yet who seemed to be always in a hurry, achieving a vast amount of confused activity without very much result. She would have looked best in tailored, rather severe clothes, but she preferred frills and draperies and plentiful jewellery. Her face was thin, sharp-featured and usually rather anxious.

"Douglas drowned!" she cried in a high, expostulating voice. "It isn't possible. We were all down there only a little while ago. He was lying around in the sun and diving and swimming about and enjoying himself. How could he be drowned?"

Douglas Cable was not her husband, he was her cousin

by marriage, but her husband, Owen Cable, Douglas's first cousin, had been dead for several years and she and her daughter Elspeth, who had lived with old Mrs. Cable since Owen's death, had been pressed to go on making the house their home when Douglas had returned from Australia to inherit Havershaw.

How the different members of the household really felt about one another was something that Catherine had not yet fathomed. The relationships between them were not close. Douglas had been taken away to Australia by his parents before Owen had married. He had never met Irene until he had come home. And Elspeth was not a Cable at all, since she was Irene's daughter by an earlier marriage. But for the present at least things seemed to be working fairly well. It would have been difficult not to get on well with Douglas, who was a boisterously generous man. Yet the atmosphere in the house, Catherine had felt recently, was not an easy one. Perhaps, she had thought, they were all working too hard at liking one another. Perhaps they had been thrown together too suddenly without any basis of understanding.

"I don't think he's drowned, I think he's going to be all right," she said, "but that's because Andie got to him in time and seemed to know what to do. Now I'm going back to the pool. You can come with me or wait here for the ambulance."

"I'll come to the pool—of course I'll come to the pool." Irene went to the door. "Mrs. Forsyth!" she called, her voice rising into a peacock scream as it always did when she got excited. "I'm going down to the pool with Miss Gifford. Please tell Miss Elspeth there's been an accident and send the ambulance men down there when they get here."

With a flutter of flowery chiffon round her thin knees, she strode out on to the terrace.

A table had been set out there with bottles and glasses.

She paused as she saw it and exclaimed, "Drinks—all you people coming for drinks and now this—I suppose it's too late to put everyone off. I mean, if we explain . . . Drowned! . . . Oh dear, Catherine, I'm so muddled, I don't see how it could have happened. Do you think it can have been a heart attack? Douglas never said anything about having a bad heart, and he looked the picture of health with that wonderful Australian tan of his that still hasn't faded, but you never can tell, can you? He may not have known himself there was anything wrong with him."

She started off across the lawn towards the grove of trees, walking with long, gangling strides.

Hurrying along beside her, Catherine said, "He could have bumped his head, diving. It was right by the diving board we found him."

"Oh, I see, yes, that sounds quite probable. What luck that you and Andie came by just when you did. If you *were* actually in time. What's the truth, Catherine? Were you in time, or are you trying to break something gently to me?"

Catherine did not answer. Her mother had died when she was fifteen, her father a year ago, but both of those deaths had been peaceful and expected, with doctors and nurses in attendance, the air full of the impersonal, chemical smells of a hospital, and with drugs to ease the parting of the spirit. The figures that she remembered lying still on white sheets had no connection with the wet thing that had briefly held her in its embrace at the water's edge, with the scents of earth and leaves around her, under the shadow of the chestnuts. Had that been death or not? She did not know.

The trees were along one side of the pool, shading it only in the evening. There was paving all round it, dotted with chairs and a few small tables. On the far side was a trellis, covered with a tangle of roses. In old Mrs. Cable's day there had been a carefully kept rose garden here, but in the spring Douglas had had some of the trees blasted out, the roses ripped up and the pool built. He had told Catherine and Andie and other neighbours to make use of it whenever they wanted. Douglas had brought an Australian sense of hospitality home with him. He liked to be surrounded by people, to feel that he was the centre of a responsive gathering. He himself swam daily, whatever the weather, and Andie often joined him. They were old friends and Andie came and went at Havershaw as he felt inclined.

He was still kneeling beside Douglas when Catherine and Irene emerged from the trees, but he was sitting back on his heels and had stopped his mouth-to-mouth life-saving effort. He was panting heavily and looked exhausted.

The figure on the paving stones was quite still. Another figure, an elderly woman who was holding a little basket of strawberries as carefully as if it were a wreath that she meant to place on a grave, was standing near them, watching with deep interest.

Irene gave a cry, "He's dead! Oh, Andie, is he dead?"

Andie pushed back his dark hair and got rather staggeringly to his feet.

"My belief is, he'll live," he answered, his tone as detached as if he himself had had nothing to do with Douglas Cable's chances of survival. "He's vomitted and he's breathing. What about the ambulance?"

"It's coming," Catherine said.

"Poor Douglas," Irene said. "Elspeth and I were down here with him only a little while ago and we told him he ought to go back with us because he'd got guests coming and he ought to get dressed, but he said there was plenty of time and that this was the best day we'd had this summer so he wasn't going to waste it. He's a very stubborn man. That's one of the first things I found out about him. He insisted on changing everything in the house straight away, I couldn't stop him. But how did it happen, Andie? He's such a wonderful swimmer. I was wondering if it was a heart attack. Or was it cramp perhaps? Or did he hit his head on the bottom when he was diving?"

"Your guess is as good as mine," Andie said. He closed his eyes for a moment, then opened them wide and looked hard at Irene. "Maybe someone who didn't like him gave him a wallop on the head and left him to take the consequences."

"Dearie, don't say that sort of thing," Frances Knox said. She was the elderly onlooker with the basket of strawberries. "With that dead-pan face of yours not everyone might realise you've a pretty good opinion of your sense of humour. You've been wonderful so far, so don't spoil it."

"I'm not joking, Fran."

"Then I'm not going to listen to you."

Frances Knox was Catherine's nearest neighbour. She had lived in the house next door to Catherine's for as long as Catherine could remember. The houses were a little way out of the village of Biddingfold on the edge of the Cable land. Frances would have come to the pool by the same path that Catherine and Andie had used a little earlier.

She was approaching seventy, unmarried, short and sturdy, with an ungirdled figure that bulged comfortably under the shapeless green and yellow cotton dress that she was wearing. She had a square, friendly, intelligent face and grey hair rolled up in a tight knot.

"Anyway, everyone likes Douglas," Irene said. "I didn't expect to, you know. I thought, a stranger coming here, because that's what he was really, a complete stranger. He couldn't have been much more than fifteen when his family took him off to Adelaide. So I thought, I'm sure I shan't like it when he comes here, we're so used to having the place to ourselves, except for Aunt Mildred, of course, but all those last years one hardly saw her. And then I couldn't help liking him, and I don't like everyone by any means. And Elspeth likes him too, which is saying a lot, because you know how critical she is."

"Elspeth's in love with him, dearie," Frances Knox said. "Hadn't you noticed?"

Irene's thin cheeks blazed. "How can you, Frances? Elspeth's engaged to Nick. You know she is, even if they won't let us announce it. They're devoted to one another."

"It wouldn't surprise me at all if Elspeth's capable of being devoted to several men all at the same time," Frances said placidly.

"Doulgas is twice her age!" Irene said furiously.

"A great attraction to some young girls, particularly those who've lost their fathers."

"Ladies," Andie said drily, "in case you hadn't noticed, our friend Doug happens to be present. To the best of my belief he's unconscious, but I'm no expert. He may be able to hear everything you're saying."

Frances chuckled. "As if he'd mind." She looked down at her strawberries. "I brought these as a little present for him. I picked them just before starting out. They're beginning to ripen at last. They're delicious. Here, Irene, you'd better take them."

"I can't, Frances—thank you, but you know it's impossible." Irene's voice began to turn shrill again. "I'll have to go to the hospital with Douglas. Someone must go and I'm the proper person. I'll go in the ambulance if they let me, otherwise I'll follow by car."

"Then you'd better have them, Catherine," Frances said, holding the basket out to her.

Just then Catherine had not the slightest desire for strawberries, but she knew that under a cheerful exterior Frances had feelings that were surprisingly easily hurt, and a tantrum or sulks, of which she was capable at the most unlikely moments, would not help the situation.

Accepting the basket, Catherine turned to Andie. "Is he really going to be all right?"

"Well, he isn't drowned," he said. "I don't think he'd been in the water more than a few minutes when we got to him. But the reason why it happened—I don't know anything about that. Could be he hit his head on the bottom and got concussion or even a cracked skull."

"Then you didn't mean what you said when you said perhaps somebody hit him," Irene said with a puzzled look at him.

Andie gave a tight little smile. The skin of his face was moulded very closely over the bones and when he smiled it was drawn into crinkles that made him look too old for his age, which was the same as Catherine's, twenty-seven. His smile was an ambiguous one, almost knowing. Andie often looked as if he knew much more than was good for him.

"There's something queer about it, isn't there?" he said. "You know how he can swim."

"But you said someone hit him deliberately."

"I only raised the possibility."

Catherine shook her head. Apart from the fact that such things did not happen in the small, safe world in which they all lived here, Irene had been right, everyone liked Douglas. You could hardly help doing so. He took vitality and cheerfulness with him wherever he went, a geniality so spontaneous that you found yourself responding to it even before you noticed his good looks.

His good looks, of course, impressed you very quickly. He had the Cable features, the high forehead and straight brows, the straight nose, the rather prominent cheekbones, the finely modelled mouth. It was a face that could have looked arrogant if, in his case, it had not been so good-natured. He was a big man, even taller than Andie and more heavily built. And even now, flat on the paving stones, with a bluish tinge on his skin and his mouth slack as he made sudden, harsh, uneven gasps for air, there was something powerful about him.

"Is that ambulance ever coming?" Irene asked impatiently. "I don't like this waiting."

"Any minute now, I should think," Catherine answered. "They said they'd come at once, but it's some distance."

"Perhaps we should go and telephone again," Irene said, "just to make sure they know where to come."

"Oh, they understand," Catherine said. "They know Havershaw. But if you like—"

"No, here they come," Andie said. "They'll have brought oxygen apparatus with them, won't they? I hope they know their job."

He moved aside to get out of the way of the men with a stretcher who came swiftly down the path through the trees.

Elspeth was ahead of them, showing them the way. Elspeth Wilde. She had never taken her stepfather's name, although she could have had no memories of her true father, who had died of meningitis when she was a baby. But Elspeth enjoyed being different from other people in as many ways as possible. She never allowed anyone to think that she was related to the Cables, or that she had any strong feelings of gratitude to the family that had brought her up.

Yet she had lived nearly all her life at Havershaw, except when from time to time she had taken a job or started training for some sort of occupation. But these spells away from her home had never lasted long. She was nineteen, a small, slender girl, with long, gleaming hair as black as her mother's, and dark eyes so large and brilliant that they dominated her rather wild little face. She was dressed now in a blue silk trouser suit and silver sandals and said nothing at all on seeing Douglas, but edged up to Irene, as if it scared her to be in such close proximity to what might be death.

Irene put an arm round her and held her tightly.

"It's all right, dear," she said. "He's going to be all right."

"We hope," Andie said.

"But what happened?" Elspeth asked rather breathlessly. "How could he drown in this little pool?"

"You can drown in a bucket of water if you give your mind to it," Andie told her.

"Be quiet, Andie," Frances said brusquely. "You only upset people when you say that sort of thing. It isn't kind."

"But what *did* happen?" Elspeth asked.

"Perhaps Brian will be able to tell us when he comes," Irene said. "Or perhaps we'll have to wait until Douglas can tell us himself. Which reminds me—oh dear, I'd forgotten—Brian was coming in for drinks and now I don't suppose he'll come. He'll probably have to go to the hospital, won't he? Anyway, I don't see how we can sit around and amuse ourselves with poor Douglas in the state he's in. It wouldn't feel right. Of course, I can't stay myself, because I must go to the hospital. Can I come with you in the ambulance?" she went on, addressing the men who had lifted Douglas on to the stretcher. "Wouldn't that be best?"

"If you like, Mrs. Cable," one of them answered. "Someone ought to come with him. There's forms and things to fill in. It'd be a help."

Andie looked as if he were about to speak, to suggest that he should be the one to go, but then was silent.

"So you see, I can't manage about the drinks," Irene said, unable to stop thinking about them. "Elspeth, you'll have to do them for me. You can do that, can't you, darling? Just in case Brian arrives after all. And then of course there's Nick too. Unless—but I really don't know what to do—would it be best to cancel everything and ask you all to go home?"

"Now listen, dearie," Frances said, "there's no need at all for all this fuss. A drink is what we all need and the obvious thing is for everyone to come along to me. I've got everything the heart of man can desire, whisky, gin, sherry, beer, Campari, Dubonnet—name it, I've got it. And I can send everyone home with a nice little basket of strawberries, if only they'll pick them themselves, because I've been gardening all day and my back's a bit tired. And Elspeth can go back to the house and wait for Nick and Brian and bring them on to me. And Andie can go home and get into some dry clothes and follow along. So go along, Irene, and don't worry about a thing."

Irene looked uncertain. So did the others. There were reasons why Frances Knox's invitations were not always accepted with the alacrity that she expected. But the men had lifted the stretcher and were starting up the path and there was no time for discussion. With the flounces of her dress rippling about her as she set off to follow them with her hasty, stumbling strides, Irene left the others to make what arrangements they chose.

Frances looked questioningly at Catherine. The old woman looked so pleased at the thought of giving a little party that Catherine had not the heart to discover suddenly that there was something else that she simply had to do.

"That'll be lovely, Frances," she said.

It meant that the others had to follow her lead.

Elspeth said, "All right, I'll go and collect Nick and old Brian. What about him, Catherine? D'you think he'll be coming or will he have to go to the hospital?"

Catherine worked part time as secretary and receptionist for the medical partnership in the district, of which Brian Walsh was the senior partner, as Catherine's father had been before him, and she knew of the comings and goings of the doctors.

She replied that it was Brian Walsh's weekend off and that he would probably be arriving at Havershaw, as arranged, and that it would be Dr. Long who would attend to Douglas.

Elspeth said, "All right, I'll wait for him," and walked away towards the house.

Andie said, "Thanks for the invitation, Frances. I'll be along as soon as I've changed."

"But remember, no more giving us gooseflesh with your sinister hints," she said, giving him a hearty slap on the back. "What happened down here was some sort of perfectly normal accident. Anything else is unthinkable."

"I'll believe it when Douglas tells me so himself," Andie muttered, and loped away in the direction of the lodge at the end of the drive which Douglas had lent to him when

Andie, soon after Douglas had arrived from Australia, had joined him in Biddingfold.

Frances stood where she was for a moment, looking after him. Her square face was suddenly troubled.

"There couldn't be anything in what he says, could there, Catherine? Of course, Douglas isn't all that he seems. I know that better than the rest of you, because I knew him so well when he was a child. But still, no one could wish him any harm. . . . No, of course not!" She chuckled and gave a little skip, an elderly child relieved from a moment's anxiety. She took Catherine's arm and they started towards her home.

CHAPTER TWO

The path which Frances and Catherine were following widened just before it reached the road into a narrow, rutted lane which separated the gardens of the houses in which they lived.

Frances lived alone in hers, but Catherine had handed over part of her seventeenth-century stone house, which was much larger than she needed, to a retired couple called Cookham, who for the sake of the very small rent that she charged them, looked after the house and garden for her. As a result her house was spotless and her garden immaculate, if rather startlingly unimaginative. Mr. Cookham had once been a cabinetmaker and valued precision. He liked to plant things in rows, flowers as well as vegetables. So the place had a geometrical, rather commercial air, as if the things in it were being grown purely for picking and for sale. He was an exceedingly skilled gardener, however, and everything that he tended flourished. Catherine never had to buy any vegetables in the village, or flowers for the house.

The house and garden next door could not have been more different. Frances refused to have any help in either. This was partly because she could not really have afforded it, but also it was because it would have given her a sense of being under observation, almost of being spied on. She felt that any woman from the village was bound to misunderstand a lot of her little ways and was certain to criticise her. So, as she grew older, she toiled hard but more and more inefficiently in the garden, helpless to prevent it turning into a jungle of unpruned shrubs, neglected fruit trees and weeds.

The house in the middle of it was a rambling bungalow, built in the nineteen-thirties but already far more decrepit than the old house next door. The paint on the doors and windows was peeling, the gutters leaked, the roughcast covering the walls was stained and dingy. But Frances was perfectly satisfied with her home, indeed, was rather proud of it, as if she had long ago stopped seeing its actual condition.

As she and Catherine turned out of the lane towards it they saw a man walking slowly towards them, pausing a moment to look curiously at the bungalow.

"Excuse me," he said as he met them, "I'm looking for Mr. Cable's house. Mr. Douglas Cable's. I was given directions in the village and arrived here, but I've a feeling I've got lost. Can you tell me if I've come the right way?"

Another Australian, Catherine thought. His accent sounded to her the same as Andie's. He was a small, stringy man and was wearing a pale grey suit with an arresting pink shirt and a tie patterned in an even brighter shade of pink and lilac. He had lost most of his hair but what he had was straw-coloured. He was the kind of man who looks unchangeably middle-aged from thirty to sixty, then almost overnight may start to look shrivelled with age, even smaller, leaner, stringier than before.

"Oh, I'm afraid you've gone quite wrong," Frances said. "It's true you can get to Mr. Cable's house this way across the fields and now you're here it may be the best thing to do, but if you've come from the village it would have been much quicker to go through the gates at the end of the drive, which almost face the end of the village street. But if you want to see Mr. Cable I'm afraid you're out of luck."

"Is he away?" the stranger asked quickly.

"Not away, not exactly," Frances said. "But I'm afraid he met with an accident this afternoon and he's just been taken to hospital. The Paxley-Parton in Newelbury. That's the town just beyond Biddingfold, you know. We haven't a hospital of our own here. We don't know how bad he is, but I don't suppose he'll be allowed visitors yet. But of course you could telephone to find out how he is, if you're a friend of his."

The stranger looked oddly angry, as if Douglas, by having an accident, had deliberately frustrated him in some way.

"What happened?" he asked. "Did he smash himself up in a car?"

Perhaps it was the roughness in his tone that affected Frances's attitude, for in the unpredictable way she had, she suddenly became wary, as if she felt that there might be some indiscretion in describing exactly what had happened.

"Oh no, nothing like that," she said.

He pressed her. "Was it a serious accident?"

"We don't know," she answered. "We haven't heard the medical report yet. But he was quite unconscious when they took him away in the ambulance. I should think at least he's suffering from concussion."

"Did he have a fall then?"

"Yes, that's right, a fall. But none of us saw it, so naturally we don't know just what happened."

Catherine could see no reason for Frances's secretiveness.

"He was by himself in the swimming pool," she said.

"Perhaps he dived and hit his head on the bottom—we don't know—anyway, a friend of his happened to be passing and pulled him out. Otherwise I suppose he'd have drowned."

The man was already looking at her when she spoke, although he had been talking to Frances. His gaze was direct, shrewd and approving.

"I see," he said. "Sounds nasty. Well, I don't suppose there's much point in going up to the house if he's not there. The Paxley-Parton Hospital in Newelbury, you said. Right, I'll telephone. I'd be sorry to miss seeing him altogether since I'm here. Not that he's expecting me, at least I'd be very surprised if he were. But I was given his name by—by someone I know—and told to drop in on him if I was in the neighbourhood."

"Then you don't actually know him," Frances said.

The man gave an abrupt, rasping laugh. "To tell the truth, I'm not sure. I'm inclined to think we don't know one another at all. But I could be wrong. Well, thank you, ladies. I'm sorry to have troubled you."

He lifted a hand briefly, turned and walked away.

Frances stood looking after him, her forehead puckered.

"Now, wasn't that an odd way to talk, don't you agree with me, dearie?" she said. "He takes the trouble to come visiting, yet he isn't even sure if he knows Douglas. Isn't that distinctly peculiar?"

Catherine thought how peculiar the man might be thinking Frances if he had known a little more about her. Knowing Frances well and being accustomed to most of her quirks, it still surprised Catherine that amongst people who hardly knew her the old woman could pass for a perfectly normal person, indeed, a very reasonable person, full of common sense, with her feet firmly planted on the ground.

Of course, all over Biddingfold it was known that she was mad. But then villages know everything and besides that like to add their touch of exaggeration to the mildest of dramas. Frances's madness was of a quite innocuous kind, harmless to herself and others, and only became fully apparent to those who entered her house. If she had kept its doors closed to the world very few people would have suspected her sanity. But she was an extremely hospitable woman and loved to herd people together in the fantastic surroundings that she called her home.

She led the way up the path now, unlocked the door and as she flung it open, called out, "Ducky, duck darlings, here's mother!"

Two dogs came lethargically trotting out to meet her.

But even before they appeared an intense smell of dog surged out at the open door. The whole house was always saturated with the smell of dog. Frances always kept her pets confined there if ever she went out, with all the windows closed in case the animals should somehow cunningly escape, get into the road and be run over.

She also kept all the windows covered with venetian blinds, because she felt a horror that some prowler might come into the garden and stand watching her when she was occupied even with such innocent things as doing the ironing or writing letters. So the house was nearly always in a state of fusty twilight and it was all too easy for someone who was not forewarned to turn an ankle on one of the raw bones that the dogs left lying about the house wherever they chose, generally in the passage or the middle of the sitting room carpet.

Just how much blood and grease from the bones had been trodden into the once fine carpet was something that

Catherine did not like to think about, but a faint rancid odour from them mingled with the pervasive dog-smell and that of stale tobacco, for Frances was a heavy smoker. But the dim light at least left partly concealed the cobwebs trailing from the ceiling and the fluff that had accumulated in corners and under chairs. On rare occasions Frances would be seized with a desire to clean her house from end to end, then the blinds would be pulled up, the windows thrown open, the vacuum cleaner would hum all day and Frances herself could be heard singing loudly yet surprisingly musically, usually Mozart arias and snatches from Handel.

One of the passions of her life was music. There were no less than three grand pianos in her long, narrow sitting room, all equally dusty, though all of them were always kept in tune. At one time, before she had become as eccentric as she had in recent years, she had given music lessons and had even taught Douglas Cable for a while, before his family had gone away to Australia. Sometimes she still urged him to take up his music again, because she was sure that he had a real though sadly neglected talent, but she played very little herself nowadays and when Catherine occasionally heard her, usually late in the evening, there was pathos in the way that the stumbling notes spoke aloud of the rheumatism in her stiff fingers.

Frances went ahead of Catherine into the sitting room, followed by the dogs, who were hoping for food. They were both cocker spaniels, castrated, fat and lazy.

"I'd better take them out for walkies," Frances said. "You know where the drinks are, dearie. Be an angel and get them out for me. And there are some packets of those cheesy things in the kitchen cupboard, only I'm not sure how long they've been there, so they may be a wee bit stale, so perhaps we'd better not bother about them.

Come along, darlings," she went on to the dogs, "out we go. We've got company coming. You'll like that, won't you?"

She shepherded the dogs out to the kitchen and Catherine heard the back door open and shut as they were taken out into the garden.

Left alone in the sitting room, she wished that she had the courage to open a window, but she knew the offence that that would give, and if ever she accidentally hurt Frances's feelings, she always felt disproportionately guilty. There was something so good-natured and so courageous about the strange old woman that her oddities aroused strong protective feelings in Catherine.

Concerning Frances's painting, for instance, Catherine had never dreamt of doing anything but appear to take it as a matter of course. Frances had begun it about ten years ago with a small pot of green paint and one paintbrush. Something had given her the impulse to paint a spray of ivy leaves on the lintel on the sitting room door. But when she had painted the spray, which she had done more skilfully than might have been expected of a novice, she had not been able to stop and ivy had soon trailed all over the door-frame, making a leafy arch of it, and then over the door itself. Then more paint had been bought and the ivy had spread to the window-frames and slowly all over the walls of the sitting room and eventually out into the passage and then had embowered the kitchen and climbed the stairs. Even the refrigerator and the cooking-stove in the kitchen and the wash-basin in the bathroom and the tiles around the bath had been decorated with luxuriant greenery.

Its likeness to ivy had fairly soon faded. With increasing practice Frances had allowed her imagination to take more and more liberties with the vegetable kingdom. Her bedroom was an orchidaceous jungle, with oddly menacing-looking flowers in flaming colours showing in great clusters through prickly, long-tongued leaves. Occasionally a human eye peeped out knowingly from the centre of some over-sized rose or daisy. When she grew tired of something that she had done, she painted it out and started all over again. Only the ceilings and the tops of the walls above the picture rails retained their original shabby whiteness, because Frances did not feel too happy standing high on step-ladders.

In the dim light the verdure on the sitting room walls had an eerie realism. Catherine had often had the feeling there that it would not have seemed strange if a snake or a tarantula had come crawling out from among the leaves. Left alone now, she happened to notice a well-chewed bone on one of the chairs. Picking it up, she dropped it into the coal scuttle. Then she went to the cupboard where Frances kept her drinks and by the time that she returned from the garden with the dogs and her first guest had arrived, the bottles and glasses were out on a tray, ready for the party.

Andie was the first to appear. He had changed into a dry shirt and trousers and had his dark hair slicked back from his face. It had an absent look as he greeted Frances and let her provide him with a drink, a look of being absorbed in some inward problem, which he often wore. But Frances was so pleased at having visitors in her house that she chattered to him excitedly without noticing how little he responded, mainly about her garden and the wonderful crop of strawberries that was ripening. She appeared to have forgotten that Douglas had ever had an accident and that his life might be in danger.

As soon as her doorbell rang again she trotted off to let

in her remaining guests and Andie moved across the room to stand close to Catherine.

"Do we have to stay long?" he asked in a low voice. "I always feel I may choke to death in here."

"You should have at least two drinks before you go," Catherine answered, "or you'll hurt her feelings."

"I could manage two drinks in a few minutes," he said, "and so could you. Then we could go to your place and talk. I want to talk to you."

"Later," she said.

"You mean that? I thought perhaps after yesterday . . ."

"Come if you want to. I haven't told you properly yet how much I like your present. I really do."

He seemed to wince, as he often did if his work was discussed.

"Throw it away, if you want to. You don't feel you've got to live with it."

He turned away from her and stood looking silently at one of the few pictures that hung on the painted walls. It was a watercolour of Havershaw, painted with a child's exuberance, colourful, bold and only just recognisable, although the effect aimed at was plainly one of simple realism.

"This is one of Doug's daubs, isn't it?" Andie said after a moment.

"Yes, I believe he painted it when he was about ten," Catherine answered. "He was a great favourite of Frances's in those days."

"About the biggest thing that ever happened to her, to go by the way she talks."

"She says there's real talent in it. Is there? I'm just plain ignorant about things like that."

"Oh, he's got all the talents. And doesn't need any of them."

Andie's voice was rather bitter. For a man who had been helped by Douglas as much as he had, he did not sound very grateful. But an hour ago Andie had saved Douglas's life. Perhaps for the moment that lightened the burden of gratitude, if it had become excessive. For it was not only that Douglas had given Andie the lodge, rent-free, to live in, but Andie only very occasionally sold one of his sculptures and that usually was to Douglas.

Frances had overheard what he had said and came trotting across the room towards him.

"Oh, dearie, how right you are," she said. "The one thing Douglas has needed in his life that he hasn't had is a little bad luck. He's got so many talents, but he's never been driven to make any serious use of any of them. He could have been a really important painter if he'd ever tried, don't you agree? Actually I've never hung up his best paintings. I don't think I could live with them. Too imaginative, too disturbing. And he was so musical when he was a boy, really far too advanced for me to teach, though I did my best for him. And he used to write me letters from school which were wonderful for a child of his age. I've kept them, they're so charming. But he never had to make any effort to excell, so somehow he hasn't turned out what I expected."

"Could you call it luck, knocking himself out and nearly drowning in his own new swimming pool?" Nicholas Redmayne asked.

He was a short, wide man, heavy-muscled and deliberate, with one of those immobile faces that look as if they have been carved out of something more unyielding than flesh. But his dark eyes were very alive, observant and restless. He was twelve years older than Elspeth, to whom he had rather unexpectedly become engaged a month ago.

Catherine, at least, had found this unexpected. She had not thought of him as a marrying kind of man. He was a travel writer who owned a cottage in Biddingfold to which he retired between his lengthy journeys to write his books. Catherine, whose part-time job did not keep her adequately occupied, supplemented it by doing his typing for him. She had some of his manuscript at home at the moment, on which she intended to do some work that evening.

"I'd call it luck, Andie arriving when he did," Brian Walsh said. "That's supposing the knock on the head doesn't turn out to be too serious."

"How soon shall we know that?" Catherine asked.

"As soon as they've done the x-rays. I'll find out and let you know as soon as I can."

Brian was a tall, rangy, slightly stooping man with a kindly, rather worn face that made him look older than the thirty-five that he was. He had been in Biddingfold for three years and because he was both skilful and a sensitive listener, had become the most popular doctor in the district. For his first two years in the village he had worked with Catherine's father, who had taught him a great deal and whom he remembered, Catherine knew, with admiration and affection.

Elspeth, who had sat down in the chair from which Catherine had removed the dog's bone, said, "Drinking here like this, it feels rather like dancing on his grave, only that I feel so sober. Poor old Douglas, I think I could drink and drink and still stay as sober as a judge all night. Is that shock, do you think, or does it mean I'm going to turn into an alcoholic?"

"I believe the sobriety of judges has been greatly overestimated," Frances said. "In the past they were noted for the amount of claret they consumed, on the bench as well as off it. And to this day, I've been told, they don't reckon it's necessary to try divorce cases sober, as they know that in any case they're going to be told nothing but lies."

"I suppose Douglas hadn't had a few drinks before he went in swimming," Nicholas Redmayne said. "Not that I suppose it would have made any difference to him if he had. He'd a very strong head."

"You said that in the past tense," Andie said sharply. "Have you written the feller off already?"

"I did?" Nick said. A shade of surprise showed on his impassive face. "Quite right, it slipped out. Unintentional, entirely. I'm sure that with that famous luck of his, we'll find his head's as hard as it's strong."

"Anyway, he hadn't had any drinks," Elspeth said. "Not since before lunch, and then I think he only had a beer. He and mother and I went down to the pool afterwards and were there nearly all the afternoon. It's been such a gorgeous day, it's extra horrible things turning out as they have. Why did they have to go and get spoilt on the very first really good day we've had this summer?"

"Now, let's not brood about it," Frances said. "Drink up, everybody." She was going round the room with a bottle in each hand, topping up glasses. "We can't help him by being miserable, so let's enjoy ourselves."

"I'm curious to know whether or not he'll remember anything about how it happened when he comes round," Brian Walsh said. "Amnesia isn't uncommon in the circumstances."

"Does it last for long, or just for a few hours or days?" Andie asked.

"Sometimes the memory never comes back," Brian answered. "I was once in a minor car smash, years ago. I wasn't even hurt, except for a few bruises, but to this day I can't remember the moment of impact."

"How very nice," Frances said. "I think it's a very comforting thought that one's mind can blot out the nastier things that happen to one. Not that mine ever has. I sometimes feel I can remember everything that's ever happened to me. It can't be true, of course, it's just how I feel. In fact, the past often feels much more real than the present. For instance, I really feel closer to the boy that Douglas used to be than to the man he is now." She gave a slight sigh. "But I suppose that's only to be expected."

The little party did not last long. Catherine and Andie were the first to leave. They strolled up the road together to the house next door. The evening sky along the horizon glowed softly with a wash of green and bronze, but overhead it was still the deep warm blue that it had been all day.

Mr. Cookham was busy in Catherine's front garden. He straightened up, smiled, said, "Good evening," and gave it as his opinion that tomorrow would be as fine as today, then he went back again to tying up some flopping carnations.

Catherine led Andy into the house, through the small, dark hall into the big, cheerful living room.

It had once been two rooms, and the division between the two rooms was still marked by a low, wide archway. A long, twisted beam, shining with the polish of several centuries, was the mantel across the top of the big, open fireplace. Catherine used one end of the room as a dining room, while the other end was furnished with some comfortable chairs, a television, some bookcases, an old mahogany bureau which was open and had her typewriter on it, and a coffee table, littered with newspapers and books from the local library.

Andie's present to her, the small, squat figure of a naked man, crouching on his haunches, was on the coffee table. He had a heavy-lidded, flat-nosed, peaceful face.

Picking the little figure up, she stroked it with the tips of her fingers.

"Yes, I really do like him," she said. "I thought I did, but it always takes me a little while to make up my mind. And I've hardly thanked you yet."

Andie had shown his familiarity with the room by automatically ducking his head to avoid the beams in the ceiling without having to be warned to do so. He looked even taller than usual in the low room, dark and straight, standing before one of the small windows set into the thick wall.

"You don't like most of my things," he said. "You don't have to tell me. You may not know it, but you've a face that doesn't hide much. They're too skimpy and stick-like for you, aren't they? Too much movement, too little repose. Aboriginal influence, probably. And it may be why I had to come to Europe, to get rid of influences and find out what I'd got in myself."

"I like things solid," Catherine admitted.

"People included?"

"Perhaps."

"I'll never be solid enough for you, shall I?"

It was true, but she hesitated, wondering what to say to him, not wanting to hurt him. The evening before he had wanted to make love to her and she had stopped him. Yet until then, for some months, she had thought of herself as in love with him. Or half in love.

As Douglas had been half drowned? What did these half states mean? Did they mean anything, considering what a gulf there was between them and the whole state?

In Douglas's case, the difference between life and death. In her case, what?

A sense of depression descended on her as she thought about this, a sense of loneliness and emptiness. Was it sheer stupidity or even cowardice on her part to reject so definitely what Andie had to offer?

Looking down at the little wooden man that she was holding, she said, "You didn't have to give me this by way of apology, if that's what it was. I blame myself for yesterday."

"I'm not blaming anybody and there was no apology about it," Andie said. "I don't apologise to people for my feelings about them. But I can't ask you to marry me, can I, if that's what you want?"

"It isn't, Andie. That's what I . . . I don't know how to say it. . . . It's got nothing to do with it."

She sat down on the sofa, which put the littered coffee table between the two of them. Then, as soon as she had done it, she wished that she had not chosen what would look like a defence. There was a crudity about it, almost as if she feared him. Yet she stayed where she was, putting his carving down again on the spot from which she had picked it up. A shaft of evening sunshine, entering through one of the small windows, lit copper glints in her hair. The pink on her cheeks brightened.

Andie drew his breath in sharply and said, "If only you weren't so bloody beautiful! And you hardly seem to know it. You don't try to make use of it. But ever since I got here I've been trying not to think about it, because I knew you'd never care for me. But how could I help it?"

"But I do care. What I'm trying to say is . . ."

He interrupted her with an abrupt laugh. "Oh, you care. Or you did until—what? Until you found me out?

Until you realised there's no stability in me, anyway of the kind you value? Until you realised I'd never be able to keep you? I hope you didn't think I wanted you because you'd be able to keep me. I'm not as greedy as that. As a matter of fact, I'm not at all greedy. My demands on life are very modest. A roof over my head, a place and time to work and enough food to keep me alive. But some day I'd be able to keep you in splendour. I believe that, even if you don't. I've a lot of faith in myself. Well, sometimes I have. There are times when the light gets a bit dim. But what's the good of talking? You've no use for me, even if you didn't know it till yesterday, because there's someone else, isn't there? Just tell me something, is it Doug?"

"No," she said.

"It isn't?"

"I told you, no."

He looked sardonic. "Then it's someone else. It's always somebody. You spend all your life being in love with someone, that's if you're normal. My guess is, it goes on till the day you die."

She wanted to stop him. He was coming too close to something that she did not want to think about.

"I'm sorry, Andie. Must we go on with this?" she said.

He laughed again. "Right, I'll say no more about it. But it's Doug, or Havershaw, or that fortune he's come into—no, that wasn't a nice thing to say. Forget it. You aren't like that. So it's someone else. You don't have to bother saying it isn't."

"You think you know so much," she said. "That's a habit you should get out of."

"Right. It's one one gets into living too much alone. There's no one to put you straight when you go wrong. Ever felt that might be happening to you too? You're much too much alone. Since, if you understand me, you aren't an artist, who needs to be."

"Not really alone," she answered. "My job keeps me in touch with lots of people. And as I've lived here all my life, I've plenty of friends."

"Friends!" he said with derision. "Like Miss Frances Bloody Knox? Not that I haven't a certain affection for the old creature. She goes her own way, which is something I admire. It's something I try to do too, hoping I'm not leaving too much of a trail of destruction behind me. I don't think I've done anyone much harm, do you?"

"Of course not."

"You'd be surprised how much I could do if I tried," he said.

He said it absently, as if he himself had been taken by surprise by the thought that he had just uttered. He turned away to the window and gazed dreamily out of it.

Puzzled, uncomfortable, and wanting to change the subject, Catherine said, "By the way, Andie, when Frances and I got back from Havershaw we met a man in the road who asked us the way there and wanted to see Douglas. I'm fairly sure he was Australian. He sounded just like you. Is he anyone you're expecting?"

He turned back to her quickly. "What was he like?"

"Small, wiry, middle-aged, bald. A very bright pink shirt and a wonderful tie."

Andie shook his head. "Means nothing to me. Well, good night, I'll leave you in peace now, and see you—well, sometime."

"Good night," she said.

He stooped, dropped a quick kiss on the top of her head, crossed the room, ducking familiarly under the low beams, and let himself out through the little hall into the gathering darkness.

He left her wondering rather unhappily why she should feel that her description of the small Australian had meant something definite to him, and something quite disturbing.

CHAPTER THREE

About ten o'clock that evening the telephone rang.

Catherine had made herself an omelette and some coffee, eaten some of the strawberries that Frances had given her and had been typing a chapter from Nicholas Redmayne's book, which was about a journey that he had made in Central Africa, living among some very primitive tribes.

He wrote entertainingly and sympathetically about the people, though it was the wild life of the continent that really put vigour into his writing. Animals, plants and the secret life of a great river seemed to mean far more to him than people. Catherine wondered if Elspeth would accompany him on his travels when they were married, or whether neither of them had considered this possibility.

It was Brian Walsh on the telephone.

"I thought you'd like to know, Douglas is all right," he said. "A bit of a knock on the head. Nothing serious."

"Is he conscious?" Catherine asked.

"Oh yes, he's been conscious for some time. But he doesn't seem to remember much about what happened. As I told you, that's common enough. But there's just one thing . . ."

She waited for him to go on. He was silent a long time.

At last she said, "Brian?"

"Sorry," he said, "I was thinking. You didn't see anything of what happened, did you—you and Andie?"

"Not till we saw him in the pool. Andie saw him first and gave a yell and went into the pool before I'd even taken in there was anything wrong."

"That's what I thought." She heard him give a sigh. "Of course the pool's screened off in every direction till you get right up to it. Even if the thing had only just happened when you got there, you wouldn't have seen it, would you?"

"You're worrying," she said. "What is it, Brian?"

"Only that the bump on his skull isn't where it ought to be."

"What does that mean?"

"It's on the back of his head. You'd think, if he dived in and hit his head on the bottom, the swelling would be on top."

She was silent, thinking it over.

After a moment he said, "Well, wouldn't you?"

"Suppose he was doing some fancy sort of backwards dive," she said. "He sometimes does that sort of thing."

"You think that's possible?"

"Isn't it?"

"Perhaps as possible as anything I've had in mind. . . ." Another pause. Brian was much given to pausing while he tried to arrange his thoughts. He was hardly ever hasty in word or action. "What I've been thinking, though I admit it's improbable, is that someone hit him. I can't stop wondering about that."

"Andie had the same idea straight away," Catherine said. "But who'd do such a thing?"

"Who stands to gain by his death?"

She felt the conversation was taking such a fantastic turn that there was no need to take it seriously.

"You know as well as I do," she said.

"I suppose I do," he said. "Irene. Elspeth. Even Nick, if he and Elspeth get married."

"Yes, old Mrs. Cable left Havershaw and half her money outright to Douglas and his children, if he has any, but if he hasn't, then it all goes to Owen's side of the family, which means Irene."

"Do you think there's any chance that Douglas has a wife and children in Australia, whom he's walked out on?"

"Well, if he has, they'd certainly have a motive for trying to drown him. But what a suggestion, Brian!" She laughed. "I don't understand what's got into you."

"You aren't impressed? Do you know there's been a man around in the village for the last few days, an Australian, asking questions about him?"

"A small, bald man? I think Frances and I have met him."

"Did he question you too?"

"Only about the way to Havershaw. He'd got a bit lost. When we told him Douglas had had an accident and been taken to hospital he went away."

"But if the man's been in Biddingfold for several days he could hardly not have known the way to Havershaw. The gates are right at the end of the village street."

"That's true. I hadn't thought of that," Catherine said. "It's odd, now you mention it."

"What did you make of him?"

"Nothing special. There was something a bit strange about the way he spoke of Douglas, as if he weren't sure whether or not they knew one another. Yet he seemed to be staying here just to see him. Have you met this man yourself?"

"No, but he buttonholed Martin in the Green Man at lunch today and asked a lot of questions that Martin found a bit curious." Martin Long was one of Brian Walsh's partners. "Which reminds me, what about having lunch with me in the Green Man tomorrow?"

"You want to meet this Australian yourself, do you?"

He laughed. "And have a little of your company. I don't have half enough of it out of office hours."

"It sounds as if you're having one of your attacks of feeling responsible for me," she said. "You really needn't."

"Look, I'm just asking you to have lunch with me. Will you?"

"Of course."

"Then I'll pick you up about twelve-thirty. I'm going along to see Andie now. He hasn't got a telephone, I can't call him, but I thought he'd like to know Douglas is all right. Thanks to him."

It was like Brian to think of doing that, Catherine thought. He had a sober awareness of the needs of others that went a good deal beyond his professional responsibilities to them.

But there were other things of which he was maddeningly unaware. Or else he preferred to appear to be. Blindness, real or assumed, was a useful defence against feelings in others which you happened not to want to encourage. He had never encouraged Catherine. When her father died he had looked after all the practical matters that would have overwhelmed her if she had had no one to help her, and it had been he who had quietly manoeuvred the Cookhams into the house, so that she should not live there alone. But he treated her with a kind of gentle caution, which was surprisingly effective at keeping her at arm's length. If it had not been for that, she would never have blundered into as close an involvement with Andie as she had. She wondered if Brian had ever realised that.

She was on duty at the morning surgery next day and was there in a white overall by nine o'clock. Brian Walsh did not come in, as this was his free weekend, but soon after she got home again he drove up to the house to collect her and the two of them set out to the Green Man.

The morning was as beautiful as yesterday's had been, tranquil and increasingly hot as the sun climbed brilliantly in the cloudless sky. Catherine had put on a dark green sleeveless cotton dress and her hair shone golden-red against it, but there had not been enough sun that summer for her arms to tan and their pallor displeased her. They struck her as looking like sticks of blanched celery. But Brian told her how charming she was looking, which was something that he seldom forgot to do. The comment came from him so regularly that she had long ago stopped feeling much pleasure at it.

They were at the Green Man in a few minutes. It was an old coaching inn, at the centre of Biddingfold, opposite the church. Ivy covered the face that it turned to the street, overlooking what had once been a handsome courtyard, but which had recently had its mossy paving-stones taken up and bald-looking grey asphalt put down to make a convenient car-park. At the same time the new management had converted the old dining room, where until recently you had been lucky if you managed to obtain sausages and bacon, or egg on chips, with tomato ketchup to help them down, into an excellent restaurant, had built bathrooms on to the half dozen bedrooms, and achieved mention in some of the more critical guides to Britain's hotels.

There had been some loss and some gain, Catherine thought, which was also true of most of the other changes in the village. For instance, the council houses at the end of it might be a blot on its charm, but Douglas's head gardener and his family, who would once have lived in the extreme discomfort of the lodge now occupied by Andie, inhabited one of the new houses, with central heating and all other conveniences, and were much the happier for it. And that left the lodge vacant for Andie, someone so wrapped up in his work that his surroundings did not matter to him.

The bar of the Green Man was a long, narrow place with walls covered with dark panelling, some of which at least dated back to the time when the inn had been built. The room was decorated with horse brasses and a good deal of blue and white china and a stuffed fox in a glass case. Catherine noticed Brian's quick glance down the length of the bar as they came in and his slight frown as he saw that the stranger was not there. She sat down on one of the benches against the wall and Brian brought sherry for them both.

As he folded his long limbs into the low chair facing her, she said, "Brian, when you phoned last night, were you serious?"

"About the possibility that someone had hit Douglas on the back of the head?"

"Yes."

"Perfectly serious, if not perfectly convinced," he answered. "You didn't seem impressed by my suspicions."

"You asked me who stood to benefit by his death and we agreed Irene and Elspeth," she said. "I don't wonder you don't feel convinced."

"Because you've known them most of your life, so naturally they couldn't have done it." He gave his slow smile. "But I agree with you, I find it hard to imagine. Not that Elspeth isn't an explosive little creature. However, there's Nick. I can easily see him being violent. In fact, to go by some of his books, he's sometimes had to be."

"But that's different from knocking a friend on the head and leaving him to drown."

"Well, we don't have to restrict our suspicions to those three, do we? And money needn't have been the motive behind it. As I said last night, we don't know much about Douglas before he came here. What do you actually know about his life in Australia?"

Catherine gave a slight shake of her head. "Almost nothing. Just that he was taken out there when he was about fifteen. His parents bought a fruit farm in South Australia and I've an impression they didn't make much of a go of it and Douglas got himself a job of some sort with a winery at a fairly early age. I don't think he ever had much money. He doesn't talk about it much. But he talked to me once about his memories of Havershaw, how it came to stand for almost perfect beauty in his imagination and how it was a wild sort of daydream he used to have that he might own it some day. And he used to plan all the changes he'd make, all the really good furniture he'd get instead of Mrs. Cable's Victorian stuff, and the swimming pool he'd have built where the rose garden used to be. I think he did a lot of reading about furniture and pictures and things, never really believing that the place was ever going to belong to him."

"But what you know is simply what he's told you."

"I suppose so."

"Did the family always keep in touch with Mrs. Cable?"

Catherine put down the glass of sherry that she had been nursing. She looked thoughtfully into Brian's face, with its expression of kindly concern. It was an expression that he was seldom without. He wore it like a mask, even when you were fairly sure that his thoughts did not really match it.

"You don't trust him," she said. "Why not?"

"It may surprise you," he said, "but my profession makes one distrustful. Your father must have told you that. So few people tell one the truth about themselves. . . ." He paused and smiled. "Here's your friend, the bald-headed man. Let's see if we can get talking to him."

He picked up their glasses, stood up and carried them back to the bar, managing to reach it so that he stood shoulder to shoulder with the small Australian, who had just come into the bar.

There followed a small battle of politeness between him and Brian as to which of them should let the other be served first, then Catherine saw them exchanging a few remarks and after a minute or two they came strolling together towards her. The stranger was in the grey suit and pink shirt that he had worn the day before. Brian introduced him as a friend of Douglas's.

"Hunnicut my name is," the small man said. "Walter Hunnicut. Your friend here had the kindness to invite me to join you—" He stopped short, his gaze suddenly concentrating on Catherine's face. She discovered that his eyes, between the straw-coloured lashes, were a slaty shade of grey. They were small, hard and shrewd and had no smile in them although his thin-lipped mouth wore a sunny grin. "You're the lady I met yesterday evening, aren't you? You and another lady. I asked you the way to Havershaw."

Catherine nodded. "Yes, and we told you about Mr. Cable's accident."

"Right. Poor bloke. But your friend here tells me he's not doing so badly." He sat down on the bench beside her. He was drinking brandy and ginger ale. "I'd only to open my mouth for him to guess where I came from and jump to the conclusion I was a friend of Cable's. Seems you don't have many Australians hereabouts."

"I'm not sure if you can call even Mr. Cable an Australian," Catherine said. "He spent his childhood here."

"I suppose he's what he feels he is," the small man said. "Of course you'd be too young to remember him before he went away."

"She was just about learning to walk," Brian said, arranging his long limbs again in the small chair facing them. "But there's an old friend from his Australian days living in the village. Perhaps you know him if you know Cable. Andrew Manson."

"I've heard about him, but only since I came here. A sculptor, isn't he? I haven't had the pleasure of meeting him." Walter Hunnicut turned his steady, cool gaze on Brian. Catherine had a feeling that he was aware that he had been deliberately picked up and that he felt some curiosity as to why this had been done. "Did he and Mr. Cable arrive here together?"

Brian looked questioningly at Catherine. "Did they? I don't remember."

She shook her head. "Andie came here some weeks after Douglas. He stayed at Havershaw for a while, then Douglas gave him the lodge to live in."

"They're close friends then," Walter Hunnicut said.

"Oh yes."

"Married? I mean Mr. Manson. I know Mr. Cable isn't."

"No, Andie isn't married."

"How's he making out here? Successful? Another great artist lost to Australia?"

There was a sneer in his voice that annoyed Catherine.

"He may be," she said. "Some people, anyway, think he's important. And I know he's got great faith in his own future. But I don't know if he means to stay here permanently or go home some day."

"I shouldn't think he knows himself," Brian said. "But one day he'll be gone and none of us will know why or where, any more than we really know why he came here."

Walter Hunnicut looked interested. "Oh, you don't know why he came?"

"I've never catechised him," Catherine said.

He gave her a swift look. "Am I asking too many questions? It's a habit we have back home. We're interested in people. We like to know all about them. But you're packed so close on top of one another here, I suppose you've got to keep your guard up or you'd be lost."

"If you're interested," Brian said, "it was Manson who pulled Cable out of the water yesterday and undoubtedly saved his life."

"Good for him. Maybe I'll look in on him while I'm staying here. Someone from home, you know. He might welcome it. He lives in that house by the gates of Havershaw, is that right?"

Brian nodded. "How long are you staying here, Mr. Hunnicut?"

"I haven't decided. I've got to get back to London sometime, but I like it here. Nice hotel, good country, a bit of the real England, that's the way I look at it. And I'm in no hurry."

"Then you aren't here on business."

"Not what you could call business."

"I expect Mr. Cable will be very glad to see you when he's recovered," Catherine said. "But yesterday you said, didn't you, that you weren't at all sure you'd met?"

Walter Hunnicut looked amused, as if he had realised that he was being asked as many questions as he had asked himself.

"Right. But we've got friends in common. We had, that's to say—once." He finished his drink and stood up. "I'll be going in to lunch now. Nice to have met you. I've enjoyed our chat. Maybe we'll be seeing each other around."

He gave the bright smile that did not reach his eyes and walked off briskly.

"What did he mean by that, that he and Douglas had friends in common *once?*" Catherine asked.

"Either that they're no longer friends or that they're dead—that seems to be the sense of it," Brian said. "What d'you think he is, a detective?"

"I don't understand what's got into you!" she exclaimed. "Why should a detective be interested in Douglas?"

"Somehow the man strikes me as acting rather like a detective," Brian said. "As the fictional type, anyway. I can't say he resembles any of the CID people I've got to know here."

"And you believe someone tried to murder Douglas yesterday, and that the roots of that are probably in Australia, and that Mr. Hunnicut knows something about it."

Brian made one of his long pauses. His kindly, slightly melancholy face was thoughtful.

"It's difficult, you know," he said, "since Douglas doesn't remember anything and says he was sure there was no one there with him. He could have slipped on the paving at the edge of the pool, slithered in backwards and banged his head as he went in."

"But you don't believe that. Are you going to tell the police your suspicions?"

"Oh, I have."

She gave him another surprised stare.

"Whom did you tell?"

"Old Sturrock."

"Did he take you seriously?"

"He listened, anyway. I think you may have a call from him sometime soon. I don't see that a little police activity can do any harm. If that was an attempt on Douglas's life, it might discourage a second try. Now, what about lunch?"

Catherine nodded, stood up and they walked through the bar to the restaurant.

All through lunch she and Brian never really left the subject of Douglas, his accident and the puzzling presence of Walter Hunnicut in the neighbourhood. She was intrigued by the way that Brian worried at it, although she would far sooner have talked of other things. He was acting almost as he did when he was unable to arrive at a diagnosis of one of his cases that satisfied him. When they had had coffee he drove her home, withdrawn by then into almost complete, brooding silence.

Sergeant Sturrock arrived about an hour after she had reached home, an hour which she had spent at her typewriter, finishing the last of the chapters that Nick had given her, which she had promised to take round to him later that afternoon. The sergeant arrived on foot from the village and spent some minutes chatting to Mr. Cookham in the garden about how his sweet peas were coming along before advancing to the door to ring the bell.

The sergeant and Catherine knew each other well. He was a tall, burly man whose stomach had gradually protruded more and more during the years that she had known him and whose brown hair had grown grizzled, but whose back had stayed straight and his shoulders square. His face was a fresh pink with a fold or two under the chin, but very few wrinkles. He had oddly shy blue eyes. He always looked embarrassed at having to question anybody, even about the most trivial matter. Yet to have believed for a moment in the embarrassment would have been a grave mistake.

Catherine took him into the sitting room, and, as he always did, he said that it was a nice room but that it didn't seem the same since her father had gone.

"Not that we mightn't have done worse than Dr. Walsh," he went on as he and Catherine sat down, and Catherine knew what was coming next. "He's been talking to me, Miss Gifford, no doubt you know about what."

"Mr. Cable's accident," she answered.

"That's right. And I've been to see Mr. Cable, who's doing well, I'm glad to say, but who says he can't remember just what happened before he fell into the water. He says he can't even remember getting out on to the end of the diving board. And he says he was alone. He spent the afternoon down at the pool with Mrs. Cable and Miss Wilde, but that they went up to the house a little time before the trouble happened, saying they were going to change because they had guests coming. And he meant to follow them in a few minutes, but thought he'd have just another dive or two. And that's when he blacked out."

"And you're making inquiries because of what Dr. Walsh told you, that the bump on his head is in the wrong place," Catherine said.

"That's about it." The sergeant's diffident blue eyes were searching hers. "And it happens that there's an odd branch lying on the ground nearby, that could have been used to hit him with."

"What does Mr. Cable himself think about it?" she asked.

"Laughs. Says who'd want to hurt him? Says he must have knocked himself out somehow. Seems quite sure of it."

"Don't you think he's probably right?"

"Probably. But Dr. Walsh isn't a man who goes about saying things he doesn't mean, is he, Miss Gifford?"

"No."

"Not an alarmist either."

"No, certainly not an alarmist."

The sergeant placed a hand on each of his blue-clad knees and seemed to be subjecting them to heavy pressure, as if to prevent himself getting to his feet and going away.

"You and Mr. Manson were the first on the scene," he said.

"Yes."

"You arrived there together."

"Yes, Mr. Manson came along from the lodge to pick me up, we went up the path to Havershaw, got to the corner near the pool, and then . . ."

"Yes, Miss Gifford?"

"He dived straight into the pool and started getting Mr. Cable out before I'd even taken in that anything was wrong."

"So for a moment you were just standing there, looking on."

"I must have been."

"But you didn't see anything, like a glimpse of someone between the trees, for instance."

She made a small gesture of uncertainty with one hand. "I don't think so. I didn't look about me, you know. It was all so sudden, I was taken by surprise. As soon as I saw what was happening I ran round the pool to help Mr. Manson get Mr. Cable out. But I've got a sort of feeling I saw some bushes waving a little, although there wasn't any wind. But I wouldn't swear to it. I could easily be wrong."

"And who was next on the scene?"

"Miss Knox. I went straight off to telephone for an ambulance and when I got back to the pool with Mrs. Cable, Miss Knox was there, looking on."

"So she must have come along the path quite close behind you. I wonder if she could have seen anything, like someone going away from the place or something like that."

"Why not go and ask her?"

"Yes, I think I'll do that. I suppose . . ."

"Yes?" Catherine said.

"I suppose she couldn't actually have been there before you."

"Standing among the trees, d'you mean, and seen Mr. Cable drowning and done nothing about it?"

He stood up. "It doesn't seem likely, does it? And I can't see Miss Knox hitting him on the head either, even though she was there on the spot. A very humane lady, worries about cruelty to animals and things like that. All the same, I mean to say, you can't help wondering, can you?"

There was no need to ask him what he was wondering about. All Biddingfold had been wondering about Frances for a long time and about what her next step might be that would take her a little further away from sanity.

CHAPTER FOUR

Later in the afternoon Catherine took the typed chapters of Nicholas Redmayne's book to his cottage in the village.

The cottage was next to the post-office and Mrs. Wells, the post mistress, kept an eye on it for him when he was away. It was of no identifiable period, having been altered too often to belong to any, and was very small, only three rooms, with a bathroom that Nick had added on the ground floor, but it was not unattractive in its unpretentious way. A clematis bloomed handsomely against the wall that faced the street, while behind the cottage what had once been a back yard, intended for dustbins and a coal shed, had been turned into a pretty little square of paving, enclosed by high, creeper-covered walls, with rock-plants thrusting up between the flagstones and with wooden benches and a table at which Nick ate most of his meals. He cooked for himself, but Mrs. Wells's daughter-in-law came in twice a week to clean the cottage for him.

He had seen Catherine coming along the street and opened the door to her before she reached it. He was in cotton trousers, a checked shirt and sandals. There was as much of a smile on his leathery, immobile face as he was capable of producing.

"Always so punctual, always so reliable," he greeted her. "What a treasure you are to have discovered in a desert like this. D'you know, if I hadn't found you, I honestly believe I'd have had to move away."

She handed him the package of typed sheets.

"Couldn't you train Elspeth, if you really can't do it yourself?" she said. "After all, she must have some interest in your success."

"Have you ever tried to keep count of the number of kinds of training Elspeth's taken up and dropped in a month? She's as unteachable as an African elephant—a simile which I hope you won't repeat to her, as she might not understand it, but actually it's one of her great attractions for me. She's basically wild and I like wild things that can't be domesticated. Now, come into the garden and I'll make a cup of tea."

He put the package down on a table in the tiny sitting room and led her through the kitchen to the little courtyard at the back.

It was almost too hot there, unshaded as it had been all day from the unfamiliarly brilliant sunshine and sheltered by the high walls from the faintest breath of a breeze. But there was a deck chair in one corner which was in the shade now, with a newspaper lying on the seat.

As Nick picked up the newspaper and folded it he said, "I haven't been doing much work today, but one has to have an occasional day off. And I've had a lot of interruptions, mainly people popping in to ask what actually happened at Havershaw yesterday. Besides which I've been brooding on it more myself than I'd have expected. Usually I'm pretty good at putting a thing out of my mind if it's distracting me, but there was something so unexpected about that drowning business that I can't stop thinking about it. By the way, Irene and Elspeth have gone along to the Paxley-Parton this afternoon to see how Douglas is getting on and when they can expect him home, and they said they'd drop in on their way back and let me know how things are. Now, sit down and make yourself comfortable and I'll get that tea. I shan't be a minute."

He retreated into the kitchen.

Catherine settled herself in the deck chair, reached for the newspaper, which was a local one, and glanced through it.

There was nothing in it about Douglas's accident. Probably it would not sound particularly dramatic to anyone who had not been on the spot, and Andie's prompt rescue of him from a small swimming pool could hardly have been made to seem hazardous or outstandingly courageous. If Douglas had drowned, that would probably have qualified as news, for commonplace as death is and over-familiar with it in its more violent forms as everyone has become through watching television, it still challenges something in the imagination. But for a rescue to be news it is preferable for at least one person to lose his life in the attempt.

Nick came out of the kitchen, carrying a tea-tray. Besides the tea and the teacups, there were some chocolate biscuits and a slab of fruitcake on the tray.

"Don't you want to look at my typing?" Catherine asked as he poured out tea for her.

"Utterly unnecessary," he answered. "I know it'll be far better than it need be, since I shall only start scribbling all over it straight away. Here, have a biscuit."

Taking one, Catherine said, "Nick, you've been in Australia, haven't you?"

He sat down on one of the benches at the table. With his sleeves rolled up and his bare elbows on the table, he looked a solid chunk of muscle.

"About three years ago," he answered. "Not for long. I'd been in Papua, New Guinea, for some months and then I did a short lecture tour in Australia and New Zealand."

Drowned Rat

"You didn't meet Douglas or Andie, did you?"

He shook his head. "Big place, Australia."

"Of course. Yet the strangest coincidences happen, don't they? So I just wondered—you've travelled so much—if you ever came across them."

"No," he said.

"Did you know there's an Australian here in the village who's been asking questions about Douglas?"

He looked interested. "Who is he?"

"He says his name's Walter Hunnicut."

"Don't you think it is?"

"I didn't mean that. But he really doesn't tell you anything about himself, except that he wants to see Douglas. Brian thinks he may be a detective."

"If he is, it probably means your friends Douglas and Andie were up to no good over there. I've sometimes wondered about that myself. Has it ever occurred to you that there's just a faint sort of possibility that Douglas could be an impostor?"

She started and asked, "How could he be?"

He grinned. "You've been thinking about it, haven't you? My question didn't shock you."

"Only because Mr. Hunnicut has made me start wondering about all sorts of things and that was one of them," she confessed. "Could Douglas be an impostor? I think Brian was thinking on those lines too when he asked me if I knew if Douglas's family had kept in touch with old Mrs. Cable. But the family lawyers would have investigated him very carefully, wouldn't they? And Frances, who used to know him so well, is quite sure of him."

"A quite dotty old woman."

"Frances isn't nearly as dotty as people think," Catherine said.

"I'd have said she's more so. In any case, she wants him

to be Douglas, doesn't she? Having him come home, having him being good to her, making a fuss of her as he has, has been one of the best things that's ever happened to her."

"But still, she can be unusually perceptive. In her way, she's highly sensitive. If he'd changed too much, or if he made too many blunders about his childhood, about which she remembers everything, I think she'd have suspected him at once."

Nick nodded. "You're probably right. I don't seriously suspect he isn't who he says he is. As you say, he must have been investigated pretty thoroughly. But talking of Andie Manson, he's really a mystery, isn't he? The one thing we know for sure about him is that he hasn't done badly out of Douglas's inheritance. He's living off Douglas, isn't he? Or that's how it looks to me. And I can't help wondering if that's because of a beautiful friendship between them, or if it's because Andie has some hold over Douglas. I admit the second seems to me the more probable."

She looked at him musingly. "You haven't many friends yourself, have you, Nick?"

To her surprise he flushed a little. "Is that relevant?"

"Only that you spend so much time wandering about the world by yourself that you can't have much need for friends. So it doesn't seem natural to you that Douglas should help Andie for any disinterested reason."

"Oh, I understand now," he said with a sarcastic sharpness in his voice. "I shouldn't have said what I did about Andie, should I? You and he—not that I'd have noticed it if Mrs. Wells hadn't insisted on chattering about it—you're quite right, I don't notice other people much—but apparently all Biddingfold's informed that you and he have got something going. . . . No." His tone changed. "Don't take any notice of what I'm saying. I'm just trying to get under your skin because you said I had no friends. That isn't a pleasant thing to be told, do you know that?"

"I'm sorry, I never thought it would worry you," she said. "I've always thought you a completely self-sufficient person who simply didn't need other people. That's all I meant. I've rather envied you."

"If I don't seem to need other people, it's probably because I've never found out how to win their friendship. Unlike Douglas, who seems able to turn a chance meeting into a lifelong friendship in half an hour. I wish I knew the trick, because then I might not get just as tired of loneliness as most people do and feel I've got to go carving my way through impenetrable jungles and writing bloody silly books about my feats just to escape from depression at my limitations. But it *is* a trick—Douglas's, you know. That's all it is. I've watched him at it."

She handed her cup back to him for more tea.

"Why didn't the trick work with you?" she asked. "Because it didn't, did it? You don't like him."

He shrugged his shoulders. "Envy? Is that a good enough reason? Also, I don't like his wallowing in his wealth as ostentatiously as he does. The way he's tarted up Havershaw, for instance. It's fantastic."

"Isn't that because he's really a rather simple person?"

"Simple people bore me," Nick said reflectively. "Perhaps that's what I've really got against him. He bores me."

"He's very generous too and he doesn't boast about it. He never talks about all he's done for Andie."

"Which brings me back to the point that there may be a very good reason why he shouldn't. And I'll tell you something else I think about those two. I may not be good at noticing what's going on in other people, but I don't believe they're friends at all. I believe there's a lot of antagonism between them."

"You weren't there when Andie went into the pool to rescue Douglas. He couldn't have been faster."

He laughed. "Isn't there a bit of difference between not liking a person much and actually leaving him to drown? There are plenty of people I don't like, but I can't see myself walking calmly off when they're drowning—particularly if I can rescue them without the slightest risk to myself."

"Why does there have to be a sting in the tail of almost everything you say?" she asked. "I was there, I helped Andie drag Douglas out. He sent me rushing off to phone for an ambulance. I saw how desperately concerned he was."

"All right, I'm wrong," Nick said. "I usually am." He cut a slice of the fruitcake, which had a slightly dry and dusty look. "Have some of this? I'm afraid it came from the post-office. No? I don't blame you." He started to eat it himself. "You've seen Brian today, have you?"

"Yes, we had lunch together."

"I ran into him this morning. I imagine he's told you his theory that someone knocked Douglas into the pool."

"Yes, and he's told the police about it too. I had Sturrock round this afternoon, asking me just what I saw."

"What are your own reactions to the theory?"

"Rather confused," she said. "Aren't yours?"

"Suppose Brian is right, who did it?"

With embarrassment she remembered that when she and Brian had been talking this over, the first person whom they had seriously considered as a potential murderer had been Nick himself. Even now she found it easier to imagine him as a person who might have given Douglas the blow that could have been fatal than anyone else she knew. She had always been aware of a streak of violence in Nick. Not that she had ever seen the violence in action. She had never seen him even mildly lose his temper. He was always grateful for the work that she did for him and considerate in his demands. In company he was generally quiet. But the violence was there, she was sure of it, deeply suppressed yet capable in some circumstances of erupting into blind destructiveness.

He was watching her with more concentration than she liked. She had a feeling that he had come pretty close to guessing what thoughts had been passing through her mind.

"What about Mr. Hunnicut?" she suggested evasively.

"Well, suppose he did it," Nick said, "why's he risking staying around here till Douglas comes out of hospital and possibly sees him and recognises him?"

"To try again, of course."

"What a nice cheery outlook you've got."

"Anyway, Brian says Douglas can't remember anything about what happened. I think Mr. Hunnicut knows that."

"But don't you think seeing him might jolt Douglas's memory?"

"That may not have occurred to Mr. Hunnicut."

"Of course, with someone like him, coming out of the blue, all kinds of motives are possible, aren't they? Douglas might have got him sacked from his job and reduced to penury, or seduced his wife or daughter, or cheated him in some important deal, or murdered his best friend, or given him away to the police for some crime he's committed, or roused just simple hatred in him. The possibilities are unlimited. Useful Mr. Hunnicut."

"In whom you don't believe." Catherine stood up. "I must be going. Thank you for the tea."

He stood up beside her. "Thank you for the typing."

They turned towards the kitchen door. "I may believe in him when I've met him myself," he said. "At the moment we can't decide, can we, whether he's a detective, a murderer, or just a lonely traveller who probably saved up for years to make this journey and now finds the only people he really enjoys seeing are fellow-Australians—"

He broke off. They had reached the sitting room and were opposite the window. Walking briskly past it in the direction of Havershaw was Walter Hunnicut.

Nick turned to Catherine. "That's him?"

"Yes."

She advanced to the door. But only just outside it she stood still. A Rolls Royce, driven by Elspeth, with Irene beside her, had turned into the village street, coming from the direction of Newelbury. It came to a stop opposite Nick's door. Elspeth sprang out of the car, threw her arms round him and kissed him warmly.

"I love that car!" she exclaimed. "I adore it. Driving it's simply heaven." It sounded almost as if she would sooner have embraced the car than Nick. "I've had it out nearly all day today, as Douglas didn't need it himself. I wish they'd keep him in hospital for weeks so that I could drive it every day."

"Darling," Irene said protestingly, lowering the window beside her, "stop chattering for just a little while, won't you? I'm sure what Catherine and Nick want to hear is how Douglas is. We've just been over to the hospital and seen him, my dears, and he's really quite himself again, though he can't remember a thing about the accident. They're letting him come home tomorrow, isn't that splendid?"

"Won't you come in, Irene?" Nick said. "Whenever Douglas's lovely monster stops at my door I feel my prestige in the village going up by leaps and bounds. And it isn't too early for a drink, is it?"

"Thank you, Nick, we'd love to stay," Irene said, "but I think we ought to go home. We've an appointment with a Mr. Hunnicut at six o'clock, and I'm afraid we may be a little late already. I don't know why he wants to see me, or anything about him except that he sounded very Australian on the telephone, and he said something about thinking he'd met Douglas sometime, so of course I didn't want to be inhospitable and I said, come and have a drink with us at six o'clock. So we ought to be going. But I thought you'd be glad to hear the news about Douglas. Elspeth, we must get on. Good-bye, my dears."

She waved a gaunt hand projecting from a ruffled sleeve as Elspeth slid into the driving seat.

"Lovely, lovely," she murmured as her small hands fell tenderly on the steering wheel. "But, Mother, I was forgetting, there's something I've simply got to tell Catherine. Catherine, do you realise Douglas is crazy about you? I didn't realise it myself till today, I only found I couldn't get anywhere with him. That's why I agreed to marry Nick, of course. One mustn't put these things off too long. But d'you know what Douglas kept saying this afternoon? 'Why hasn't Catherine been to see me? Why didn't you bring her? Doesn't she know she's the one person I want to see? Why does she keep away?' Oh, it went on and on. It was a revelation. He's besotted."

"Darling," Irene said, "I really do think—"

"Yes, all right."

Elspeth gave a radiant smile at Catherine and Nick, then with a look of uncomplicated joy on her face she gave her attention wholly to the car and drove off down the narrow street towards Havershaw.

Standing on his threshold, Nick burst out laughing.

"She's got no sense, no manners, no discretion, and she'll never learn— Oh, I love her!" he said.

"Well, let me know when you want some more typing done," Catherine said, and set off after the car towards her home.

Elspeth's nonsense had made her feel both amused and on edge. She had never seen any trace in Douglas of more than a good-humoured liking for herself and it had never occurred to her to want more. If he wanted specially to see her now, she thought, it was probably simply to thank her for the help that she had given Andie in pulling him to safety. Passing the gates at the end of the drive to Havershaw, with the little Gothic lodge inside them, where Andie lived, she had an impulse to go in to see him, because they at least now knew where they were with one another. But instead she went on along the road past Frances's bungalow to her own home.

Frances was in her garden, snipping dead blooms off the rose-bushes that stood almost lost amongst tall clumps of willow-herb. When she saw Catherine she came to the gate, followed lethargically by her two dogs. A cigarette was stuck to her lower lip, which was almost permanently marked with a brown smudge of nicotine.

Leaning on the gate, she asked, "Have you heard any more about how Douglas is, dearie?"

"I've just seen Irene and Elspeth, who'd been to the Paxley-Parton," Catherine answered, "and they said he'll be home tomorrow."

"Well, isn't that splendid?" Frances said. "But I tell you what—" She was looking troubled. "I think you and I must co-operate to squash this idea that's going around that what's happened to him was anything but an unfortunate accident. As it certainly was. Andie started the trouble, didn't he, straight away up there by the pool?

Drowned Rat

And I've sort of felt it in the air wherever I went when I did my shopping this morning. It's the sort of idea that can do a lot of damage. It can linger on and make people suspicious of one another and turn into a kind of legend that lasts for years and years. So if anyone tries talking to you about it, just say it's all nonsense, you were there yourself and you know for certain it was just an accident."

"Let's wait to hear what Douglas himself has to say when he gets home," Catherine said. "So far, it seems, he doesn't remember anything."

"Have you seen him then?" Frances asked.

"No, but that's what Irene told me and so did Brian."

"Well, that's a pity in a way, isn't it? It's the sort of situation on which rumours can feed. Not that I see Douglas himself encouraging them. If he doesn't remember anything, he'll assume it's because there's nothing to remember. Why haven't you been over to see him?"

"Well, I was sure Irene and Elspeth would be going and I didn't think he'd want too many people at the same time."

"Poor boy," Frances said. "You do agree with me, don't you, that Elspeth's in love with him? If that child's capable yet of what one would call love. But certainly she's infatuated. I've often wondered what he said that made her go and get engaged to Nick. Because she doesn't give two pins for him, that's perfectly obvious. I feel very sorry for him. But what I think is, Douglas must have said something really cruel on purpose to try to bring her to her senses."

"Perhaps he told her she was never to drive the Rolls again," Catherine suggested.

Frances tittered. "Oh dear, how stupid you think I am, don't you? But I'm not, you know. I notice a great deal. About Douglas, for instance. I understand much more about him than most of you do, and that isn't only because I knew him as a child, though that helps, of course. He isn't at all the simple, uncomplicated person that most of you think he is. Oh no, not at all. But I mustn't keep you gossipping. Come along, ducky, ducky darlings"—she turned to her dogs—"you and mother had better get on with some gardening, hadn't we?"

CHAPTER FIVE

Because next morning was Sunday and she had no need to go to the surgery, Catherine got up later than usual, put on a dressing-gown, made her breakfast of coffee and toast and took it out on to the terrace that ran along the back of the house, to sit on the swing-seat there and enjoy the sunshine.

The day was as bright as the last two had been. The stillness of it produced the illusion that it was virtually impossible for the weather ever to change. From some trees beyond the garden wall came a cooing of wood-pigeons. Catherine enjoyed the husky repetitive sound. But Mr. Cookham waged a war to the death against the birds because of what they did to his vegetables. He had a system of strings that went criss-cross all over the garden, to which tightly folded sheets of newspaper were attached, which fluttered in the breeze and were believed by him to frighten the pigeons away. The newspaper did not add to the beauty of the garden, but Catherine had long since decided not to interfere with anything that he did there. His undisputed sway over it gave the old man a great deal of pleasure and saved her a great deal of trouble.

She had finished her toast and was drinking her second cup of coffee when Mrs. Cookham emerged on to the terrace. She was dressed for church in a vivid blue and white two-piece, a shiny blue satin hat more or less in the shape of a tea-cosy, white gloves and white sling-back shoes with far higher heels than she ever wore on a weekday.

"There's a gentleman wants to see you, dear," she said. "He rang our bell by mistake instead of yours, but I've taken the liberty of putting him in the lounge. I didn't realise you weren't dressed yet. Shall I tell him you can't see him? He's a Mr. Hunnicut."

Catherine stood up. "No, I'll see him." She picked up her tray to take it back to the kitchen. "Would you mind telling him I'll be a few minutes? And perhaps you could bring him out here to wait. It's such a lovely morning, it's a pity to stay indoors."

She went into the kitchen, put the tray beside the sink and went upstairs to dress.

When she came down again she was wearing her dark green cotton dress and a pair of small opal ear-rings. She found Walter Hunnicut sitting comfortably with his feet up on the swing-seat. He sprang up as soon as he heard her footsteps on the paved terrace.

"I must beg your pardon for disturbing you," he said. "I didn't think. I should have come later."

"Or I should have been up earlier." Catherine sat down on the swing-seat and gestured to him to sit down beside her. "What can I do for you? Would you like some coffee?"

"No, thank you, nothing." He sat down and while he smiled at her, observed her with his expressionless, slaty grey eyes which never reflected his smile. "I've been told Doug Cable's coming home today," he said.

"So I've heard."

"Then he wasn't much hurt."

"Luckily, no."

"Luckily, as you say." He had begun to swing the seat gently. It moved faintly backwards and forwards, stirred by his foot on the paving. "Next time he might not be so lucky. Has he told you how it happened?"

"No, he still can't remember. Mr. Hunnicut—" Catherine brought the swinging seat to a standstill by a slight stiffening of her ankle. "What is it you really want to know about Mr. Cable?"

"Ah," Walter Hunnicut said. "Well." He put the tips of his fingers together and looked at them thoughtfully. Then suddenly he turned his head and looked intently at Catherine. "Excuse the question, but did Cable give you those ear-rings?"

Her hand went up to touch one quickly, as if to remind herself what ear-rings she was wearing.

"No," she said.

"Did Manson?"

"No."

"Neither of them?"

"I've just told you so, haven't I?"

He clicked his tongue. "I'm sorry. Impertinent questions. It's just that most opals come from Australia. I couldn't help wondering."

"I've had these for years," Catherine said. "I don't know where they came from originally, but they were my mother's and she left them to me when she died. She died when I was fifteen."

"I'm sorry," he said again. He looked confused, as if he did not know how to go on. "Anyway, perhaps you don't know either Cable or Manson well enough for them to be giving you presents."

"Mr. Hunnicut, you haven't answered my question," Catherine said. "What do you really want to know about Mr. Cable?"

He sighed uncertainly and as if he were choosing his

words with great care, replied, "I suppose you could say I'm conducting an inquiry."

"Are you a policeman?"

He gave a laugh. "Policemen don't come my size where I come from. I'm short of about six inches."

"A detective then? A private detective?"

He shook his head. "I'm conducting the inquiry purely on my own account."

"Well, how can I help you?"

He hesitated, then took a wallet out of a pocket and with careful fingers extracted two photographs and handed them to Catherine. They were colour prints. One was a snapshot of the head of a young woman with chestnut hair falling around her shoulders, grey-green eyes, an oval face and what looked like small opal studs in her ears. The other was a photograph of the same girl, kneeling on the ground with a background of trees behind her and holding a large frying pan with several sausages in it. A little way behind her, drinking deeply from a mug, was a barefooted little girl of about three years old, with hair of the same warm golden-brown as the young woman's.

Catherine studied the photographs carefully for a moment, then said, "Yes?"

"You remind me of her a little," the man said. "Your hair's the same colour."

"And the ear-rings," she said. "I see why you asked me about mine. At least—I suppose I do. But if you look carefully, mine are round, hers are oblong."

"Yes," he said. "Yes, of course, I should have remembered that. It shows how quickly one begins to forget things." He closed his eyes for a moment as if he were trying to call up some image beginning to grow dim. "I suppose I knew it all the time really, but I couldn't stop myself asking."

"Who is she? Your wife?"

"That's right."

"And the little girl?"

"Coral. Our daughter. We were on a picnic one Sunday afternoon in a nature reserve near Adelaide—that's where we live, near Adelaide—and I snapped them both."

"But why did you want me to see these photographs, Mr. Hunnicut?"

He reached out and took them from her and put them back into his wallet.

"They don't mean anything to you, do they?" he said.

"I'm sorry—no." She had heard the extreme tension in his voice as he asked the question, though he had tried to mask it with casualness. With more sympathy for him than she had felt at first, she had begun to guess where his inquiry was leading. "Has she left you?"

He gave a brief nod.

"And you thought perhaps it was for Douglas Cable."

"I didn't know of anyone else it could be. There was something someone said about having seen them together several times when she'd told me she'd gone to stay with a friend. So when she vanished I went looking for him. But of course I couldn't find him till someone told me he'd come into money and gone off to England. And when I found out where he was it was some time before I could get away. There was Coral to think of, you see. I had to make sure she was being properly looked after."

"Your wife just left you then, without telling you anything about where she was going?"

"Yes, she didn't even leave a note behind to tell me we were through, and that it would be best to leave it at that. Which is what I might have done if it hadn't been for Coral. A child needs a mother. Things have been going wrong with the kid ever since June left. She's got nervous, has nightmares, tells lies, has fits of screaming rage so that I'm worried for her reason. And she used to be the happiest little soul in the world."

The seat that they were on was swinging again gently as he talked.

"I'd never realised June wasn't satisfied with our life," he went on. "Of course, she was a gay one, she liked parties, she liked going out much more than I did. Perhaps, I've sometimes thought since she left, she married too young and I was too old for her. She'd have been happier if she'd seen a bit more of the world before she settled down. . . . Look, Miss Gifford, I don't know why I'm telling you all this. I came to show you those photographs and ask you if you'd ever seen her here."

"Have you shown them to anyone else in Biddingfold?" Catherine asked.

"No," he said. "I didn't much want to show them to anyone, that's the truth. So I've just been asking questions. But it wasn't getting me anywhere. So I thought perhaps that was because I was afraid of coming straight out and asking what I wanted, showing that photograph and saying, 'Have you ever seen her around?' But you don't think she's ever been here?"

"I honestly don't. Mr. Cable arrived here alone and I can't remember ever hearing him speak of any girl he was involved with in Australia. Are you going to wait to see him and ask him about her?"

"You bet I am!" The knuckles in his brown hands showed white. "Because even if she never came here with him, he may know what's happened to her. Not that I care all that much for my own sake, as I told you. If I'd only myself to consider, I'd let her go. But there's Coral, the poor kid, getting all twisted up through no fault of her own. . . . Oh well, I've taken up too much of your time." He got to his feet. "I must go."

Catherine stood up too. "I wish I could help," she said, "but I'm awfully afraid you've come on a wild goose chase."

"Yes. Maybe. Well, thanks for listening. I appreciate it. Good-bye."

At the door he gave her a hard handshake and went off down the road towards the village.

When he had gone Catherine washed up her breakfast things, then went to her room and changed into her swimsuit and the loose shirt that she usually wore over it when she walked across the fields to the swimming pool. Approaching it today, she found herself noticing with a thoughtfulness that she never had before how completely concealed it was, both from the meadow and from the house, until you were almost upon it. That privacy gave the place great charm. Douglas had designed it carefully. But suppose you were alone there and it just happened that you had an enemy, how easily you could be at his mercy.

But why suppose any such thing? Why let yourself become infected by this thing that was in the air and that Frances had warned you against the evening before, that there might be something suspicious, something sinister about Douglas's accident?

She had the pool to herself. At first she found it faintly ghost-ridden, as if eyes were watching her from amongst the bushes and as if some enemy of her own, whose existence she had never suspected before, were about to show himself to her in some terrifying form. But when she looked straight at the spot from which the secret gaze seemed to be coming, there was nothing there. No twig crackled suddenly under a cautious footfall. No leaves stirred inexplicably in the windstill air. A blackbird was singing a song of joy and triumph and the roses on the trellis scented the air. Soon the ghosts were defeated and it was with a sense of peace and well-being, about an hour later, that she strolled home again to her lunch of bread and cheese.

She did not see Douglas until five o'clock that evening. He came by the path across the fields and stopped for a chat with Mr. Cookham in the garden before he rang the doorbell. Catherine had heard his voice outside, a deep, resonant voice that carried without his having to raise it, and was opening the door to him just as the bell pealed.

He smiled and said, "You were waiting for me! That's a thing to put the heart back into a poor invalid, to have a lovely girl listening at her door, ready to throw it open the moment he arrives."

There was no Australian in his accent. It had remained what it must have been when his parents had taken him abroad.

"You don't look like a poor invalid," Catherine said. "You're looking very well. I'm so glad, Douglas."

In fact, he was rather paler than usual and there was something slack about his shoulders as he followed her into the house, as if the short walk down from Havershaw had tired him. The strongly modelled Cable features seemed to be more fine-drawn than usual. But his smile had as much warmth as always and his gaze, its directness.

"I'm quite all right," he said. "But why didn't you come to visit me in the hospital? When visiting hours came round yesterday I expected you, but you didn't come."

"Didn't Irene and Elspeth go to see you?" Catherine said. "No one in hospital really wants too many visitors at a time."

"But do you have to be told whom I'd sooner have seen? Oh, they meant to be very good to me. Irene fluttered as usual and Elspeth did her best to eat me up, as she always does. Catherine, someone's got to protect me from that child. I'm not cut out to be a father figure."

He had sunk down into a chair beside the big empty fireplace. His long legs seemed to stretch a surprising way across the hearth-rug.

"I thought Nick would be able to cope with her," he went on. "But d'you know why she really got engaged to him? It was because I insulted her. I told her she was a child and that my taste didn't run to children."

"She's nineteen," Catherine said. "That isn't young for marriage nowadays."

"Marriage!" he exploded. "Who's talking of marriage? Anyway, she's a very immature nineteen. But it appears she was bitterly hurt by what I said and next day, yes, I assure you the very next day, she produced a fiancé, just to show that she didn't seem like a child to everybody. But what's a fiancé, after all, once you've proved your point? Nick's a tough sort of character and I suppose he cares for her, but it's not going to surprise me any day now to hear the engagement's been broken."

"D'you know, you're vainer than I thought," Catherine said. "Can't Elspeth be worried about you when you nearly drown, without being in love with you?"

"It isn't vanity, it's desperation," he said. "And you didn't come to see me when you must have known how I'd want it. Why didn't you? Have I annoyed you?"

"Of course not. But as a matter of fact, I didn't know you'd feel this rage to see me. Now, would you like a drink, or would that be bad for you?"

"Good or bad, I'd like one very much."

"Whisky?" It was his usual drink.

"Please," he said. "Catherine—"

She had gone to the tray of drinks on the sideboard at the other end of the room. She paused and looked round at him. "Yes?"

"Why shouldn't I want to see you? Want it badly?"

"It's so new," she said. "Well, isn't it? I can't help feeling it might be an after-effect of that knock on the head."

"Ah yes, that knock," he said thoughtfully. "I've been told so much about it and I don't remember a bloody thing myself. Brian thinks someone tried to murder me. Seems he doesn't find it surprising that someone should want to. The other doctor, Long, thinks I slipped on the diving board and hit the back of my head against it somehow as I went in. I must say, I prefer that theory."

"Is your head still painful?"

She brought his drink to him and sat down facing him.

He explored the back of his head with the tips of his fingers.

"It's somewhat sore. Not too bad. I've been having headaches, but that's all. Catherine darling, you helped pull me out, didn't you? Irene told me all about it."

"I tried to hold on to you while Andie was doing the hard work," she answered. "You're a terrible weight, do you know that?"

He looked down at his own length, sprawled in the chair.

"I'm sorry. And all the more grateful. And wouldn't mind repeating the experience. D'you think that's why I wanted you to come to the hospital so badly—that I'd a sort of half-memory of what happened and thought it was pretty good?"

"I think you were flat out and didn't know a thing. Did Andie go to see you?"

"Good old Andie—no. I haven't seen him yet. I haven't

thanked him. Catherine, I know you must be dead bored with questions now, but would you mind just a few more? Would you mind telling me what actually happened? It's a peculiar feeling having been the central figure in a drama and not knowing a thing about it?"

"I shouldn't think there's anything I can tell you that you haven't been told already," she answered. "We were coming up to have drinks with you—do you remember that? And Andie came and called for me and we walked up to Havershaw together. And we got to the point where the path goes close to the pool and there you were. Andie saw you first and was in the water before I'd realised what was happening, and he got you out and stayed with you and gave you the kiss of life while I ran off to phone for an ambulance. Is there anything else you want to know?"

"Not if that's all that happened."

"I think it is."

"You didn't see anyone near the pool on your way there, or while you were getting me out?"

"So you *are* worrying. . . . No, I think I saw some bushes waving as if someone had brushed past them, but I'm not really sure, and the only person who arrived before I got back to the pool with Irene was Frances. You can't see Frances knocking you out, can you?"

"I wonder. No, I suppose the thought's a bit too bizarre. Anyway, we're great friends, Frances and I. But I've been told something curious that I don't much like the sound of myself. There's an Australian in the village, a man called Hunnicut, who appears to have been going around asking questions about me. He went to see Irene yesterday evening and he asked her what she knew about my circumstances in Australia. And Brian told me the man's been talking to him too, also asking questions. Well, I don't know anyone named Hunnicut and the description that both Irene and Brian gave me doesn't mean a thing to me, but I don't like the feeling that there's someone around who's deliberately trying to stir up mud about me for no reason that I can understand."

"He's been here," Catherine said. "He was here this morning. He seemed to be trying to find out if you'd made off with his wife."

Douglas made a sardonic grimace. "And you believed him?"

"Why should I?"

"But why should he think you'd know anything about it?"

"I don't know. He showed me a photograph of her. I thought at the time he just needed to talk about her."

"But of course you'd never seen her."

"No."

"No, of course not. But I don't like it. I wonder if he's got me confused with somebody else, somebody who did make off with his wife and it's left him a bit unhinged."

"Unhinged enough to knock you into a swimming pool and leave you to drown?"

"Isn't it as good a theory as any?"

The doorbell rang.

"Expecting anyone?" Douglas asked. "Shall I go?"

"No, I don't know who it is. Anyway, don't go." Catherine went to the door.

It was Andie. From the doorway he could see through the little hall into the living room, to where Douglas lolled by the fireplace.

"So he's here," he said, sounding put out by the discovery.

"Come along," Catherine said, taking him by the arm. "You'll have to let him thank you sometime. You may as well get it over." She drew him into the living room. "Here's your rescuer, Douglas, and he's unfamiliarly overcome with shyness, so I'd keep my thanks to a minimum and concentrate on having a drink together."

Douglas got to his feet. He had picked up Andie's little wood carving from the coffee table.

"Hallo, Andie," he said.

"Hallo."

"Is this something of yours?"

"Yes."

"Nice."

"Thanks."

"Hell, it's my job to say thank you, not yours."

"Forget it."

The two men were standing several feet apart, each curiously stiff in his attitude.

"I try not to forget what I owe," Douglas said. There was a surprising lack of friendliness in his tone.

Andie shrugged his shoulders. "If you want to pay me off, Doug, you know there's one way you can do it."

"What's that?"

"Keep away from Cath. Just that. Then you really can forget everything else."

Catherine was so startled that she looked from one to the other in bewilderment, unable to take in what was happening. Was Andie trying to pick a quarrel with Douglas over her?

Andie's rigidity, she suddenly realised, was not at all the product of embarrassment, as she had thought at first. It was the sign of an intense anger. Under scowling brows his blue eyes blazed.

At the same time Douglas's stiffness had something strange about it. It seemed unlikely, because he was much the bigger and more confident of the two men, yet he looked almost afraid of Andie.

Catherine remembered suddenly what Nick had said about there being more antagonism than friendship between the two men.

"That's something for Catherine herself to decide, isn't it?" Douglas said, not quite steadily.

"I could make her decide pretty quickly if I wanted to, couldn't I?" Andie answered.

"But what would you gain by doing that? Not her gratitude. I don't think you'd get much of that."

"My own satisfaction, then, a bloody lot of satisfaction."

"Which you might find came rather expensive."

"But don't you sometimes want something expensive, Doug, something that's way, way beyond anything you can afford?"

"I'm glad you realise you can't afford it."

It seemed to Catherine that they had forgotten that she was there, listening to them.

"But just remember it could come far too dear for you too, Doug—even for you. A lifetime too dear."

"For you too, Andie, for you too. Don't ever imagine it wouldn't."

"Whatever are you both talking about?" Catherine broke in. "I'm appalled at you. I thought you were going to slap each other on the backs and mumble thanks and then settle down and have a drink together. And here you are quarrelling, and I don't understand what about."

"About you, of course, darling," Douglas said. "Didn't you notice Andie didn't like finding me here alone with you? You're the one thing we can't bring ourselves to share. And Andie seems to think my debt to him gives him the right to ask me to get out of his light. But that's something I'm only ready to do if you ask me to."

"I don't believe it," she said. "You sounded as if you were threatening one another."

"Don't worry, Catherine, Andie and I often have our little scenes," Douglas said. "Have you never seen one of them before? But after this one, Andie, I think we'd better go, or next time we'll neither of us be welcome here. Catherine isn't as used to your temperament as I am. Have you really never run into it, Catherine? It usually comes on when his work hasn't been going too well. He's filled with hate of the whole world and particularly of his best friends. I've seen him come near doing murder when the fit's on him. Come along, Andie, let's get going."

Catherine half expected some kind of explosion from Andie, but with a sullen frown on his face he let himself be led away. She followed them to the door and watched them as they went down the path together. Douglas made an attempt at friendliness, putting an arm across Andie's shoulders, but Andie shrugged it off. Douglas put his hands in his pockets and they walked away side by side in silence.

CHAPTER SIX

As she closed the door, Catherine had a battered feeling, fretful and scared. Did other people's emotions always scare her, she wondered. Could she only tolerate calm, stability, mildness?

Certainly this had not always been so. When she had been Elspeth's age she had had a temper that could flare up with devastating suddenness and she had been able to feel passionately about people, often astonishingly different kinds of people, with excitement, joy or pain. Looking back, she thought that she had had a stormier and more erratic set of emotions than the average.

So what had changed her? Was it the death of her father, or the year before it, when she had been almost wholly absorbed in looking after him? That time had affected her deeply, yet not, she thought, in the way of driving her emotions underground. What had done that? Once she had got over the worst of her loss, why should she have altered?

For the truth was that she had altered so much that a quarrel of the kind that had just happened in her living room, a quarrel which after all had been very restrained, very brief, and had not even got as far as abuse, let alone anywhere near violence, left her not merely on edge but filled with this puzzling fear.

Exasperated with herself because of the way that she had reacted to those few moments of tension, she finished the drink that she had poured out for herself and went to the kitchen to carve some of the cold beef that had been in the refrigerator for the last day or two and make a salad.

Next morning, after an uneasy night, she was wakened by the telephone ringing beside her bed. It was Frances.

"Dearie," Frances said, "I know I oughtn't to ring up as early as this, but I know you'll be off to work soon. Please, dearie, would you be an absolute angel and help me out of an awful mess I've got into?"

Catherine propped herself up on a pillow, preparing to listen for some time.

"If I can," she said. "What's the trouble?"

"It's my strawberries. It's really terrible. It's never happened to me before. It's the awful cold summer we've had and then suddenly this heat wave. They're all ripening at the same time. I've been along the rows this morning and there they are, all looking gorgeous and all wanting picking immediately. If I leave them till tomorrow they'll spoil. And to make things worse, my back's giving me hell—real hell, dearie. I know I've overdone things in the garden recently and it's all my own fault, because I know that sooner or later I always have to pay for it, but I've got to try and keep things under control, haven't I? So I started wondering—only of course say no if it's at all inconvenient—if you could come along for a bit and help me pick. I thought I'd ring Elspeth too and see if she'd help. You're both strong young things. And then there are the Cookhams. You could tell Mrs. Cookham she can have all she likes for making jam—I'm sure she's the sort of woman who makes lots of jam, in fact, I can remember her giving me some of her quince jelly last year and very good it was too—and I thought if there are still too many to share out among my friends, I could put a table by the roadside and sell them to people going by in cars. I could look after that, because of course I shouldn't have to do any stooping, and it would really be rather fun. I think I'd enjoy it. But the first thing is just to get the strawberries picked. Do you think you can possibly help me?"

"Of course, but I shan't be able to get there till about twelve o'clock," Catherine said. "I've got to go to the surgery as usual."

"Oh, I know that. I wasn't expecting you any earlier. But you'll come when you can manage it?"

"Yes, as soon as I can."

"Dearie, that *is* so good of you. I'm really grateful. And don't bother about lunch. While you're doing the hard work, I'll get something nice ready for us, and I've got some cider and we'll have it in the garden and we'll all have lots of fun. I wonder what price I ought to charge at the roadside. I don't want to give the strawberries away for charity, I think I may as well try to make a little money while I'm at it. If you're going into the village, you might see what they're charging in the post-office, then I'll charge a little less. Now I'll ring Elspeth and see if I can rope her in too."

Frances rang off.

Catherine got up yawning and went to have her bath.

It was Brian's surgery that morning and a very busy one. A good many of the patients in the village chose to wait for the days when they knew that they would have his attention, rather than that of Dr. Long or either of the other two doctors in the partnership, and when Brian had had a free weekend the queue waiting for him on a Monday morning was always longer than usual.

Then afterwards, before he set off on his round of visits, he wanted a word with Catherine. She was busy returning the patients' record cards to their files.

"Have you seen Douglas yet?" he asked.

"Yes, he came to see me yesterday evening," she answered.

"To say thank you, I suppose."

"Yes, and to ask me if I'd seen anything odd on the way to the pool that evening."

"So he still can't remember anything about it."

"Apparently not."

"That's curious."

She was puzzled. "But you said it was almost to be expected."

"Yes, I did. That's correct."

"So what's curious?"

"Just an impression . . ." He made one of his long pauses, giving her an abstracted look. "I could easily be wrong, but I've got an odd feeling it may have been I myself who put it into his head that it might be convenient to forget what happened. But these tricks of memory are always intriguing. Those few minutes, whatever happened in them, may be genuinely lost to him for ever, or they may suddenly come back when he's least expecting it. Or, just possibly, they've never been lost. If he saw someone he really wanted to protect, for instance . . ."

"Actually, he did mention Frances, and then said quickly it couldn't have been her."

"As a matter of fact, I've been thinking of Frances myself. She's quite strong, you know. Though why she should want to. . . . Anyway, I'll be interested to hear if the memory ever comes back."

Carrying his black bag, he went out to his car.

Catherine finished the work of filing the cards and tidying up, then went home, changed into slacks and a shirt and set out to help Frances with her strawberries.

The patch of them was surprisingly large for a garden

the size of Frances's. At one time in her life she had launched out into soft fruits, strawberries, raspberries, loganberries, blackberries, meaning to market them in Biddingfold and Newelbury and make a little money. But since she had never had any intention of employing labour and since even then her back had begun to trouble her, the project had been doomed from the start. Where the blackberries had been carefully planted out against wires, there was now only a great prickly tangle of brambles, many feet thick. The loganberries had quietly given up the ghost. Halfheartedly the raspberries survived and gave Frances a few pounds for bottling each year. Only the strawberries somehow flourished.

But the crisis this year was unusual. Generally Frances was able to keep pace with the picking herself and every day or two would appear on the doorstep of some friend carrying a punnet prettily lined with strawberry leaves and generously filled with fruit, and at the most would accept a glass of sherry in return and of course a pleasant half hour of gossip. But this year the exceptionally cold May and early June, followed by the blazing sunshine of the last few days, had created an almost unprecedented situation. The strawberry plants were weighted down with fruit, even larger and more luscious than usual, and all ready to be picked at the same time.

Taking one of the punnets which Frances had produced from somewhere in the bungalow, Catherine went to work, straddling a row of plants and snipping the strawberries off neatly between finger and thumb and gently arranging them in the little square basket, so that they should not be bruised. Then she filled another. Elspeth, working her way down another row, stood up when she saw Catherine, rubbed the small of her back and gave a groan. Her vivid little face was flushed from stooping.

"D'you know what I'm going to do when this is finished?" she said. "I'm going to take a nice pile of cushions to the pool and lie down with them wedged under my bottom till the kink in my spine's been ironed out. I feel as if it might take several hours."

Frances overheard her.

"Dearie, don't tell me your back's hurting you," she said. "If it is, you must stop at once. Once you've strained your back, you know, you're stuck with it for life. That's what happened to me. I used to be immensely strong, I still am, if it comes to that. But how I have to pay for it if I do anything stupid."

Anything as stupid as, for instance, hitting a man on the head and leaving him to drown in his own swimming pool, Catherine suddenly wondered. Then, taking a look at Frances's broad, smiling face, wondered how such a preposterous idea had ever come into her head.

"So if your back's really hurting you," Frances went on, "stop picking and come and help me get lunch."

Elspeth, who would sooner have picked strawberries all day than do anything in the least domesticated, laughed and said, "Don't worry, I'm only complaining on principle. Actually, I'm rather enjoying myself. You don't mind me eating about as many as I pick, do you? It's just been dawning on me, I've never really had enough strawberries to eat in my life before."

"Eat all you can, dearie—of course you're welcome," Frances answered. "Just so long as they don't upset you. Too many can have a shattering effect on the bowels. I speak from experience. Living alone, you know, one either becomes greedy about food, or stupidly indifferent. My vice is greed. I honestly love my food and in the strawberry season I overeat atrociously. Which reminds me, it's time I went to get our lunch, so I'll leave you for the present. It's nothing much—just a cold collation. Isn't that a lovely phrase, a cold collation? It makes one think of embroidered tablecloths spread on the grass near gurgling streams, and footmen with silver buttons on their liveries, and ladies in hats, and roast pheasant and the popping of champagne corks. None of which you will expect. But I don't want you to starve, so forgive me if I leave you for a little."

She trotted off into the house.

Elspeth stood upright again. "There won't be an embroidered tablecloth, but there'll be something gorgeous," she said, "and there'll be twice as much as we want and her feelings will be hurt if we don't eat it all."

She and Catherine were the only two pickers who had arrived. Catherine had asked Mrs. Cookham to help, forgetting that Monday morning for her was as sacred to doing the washing as Sunday was to going to church. Mr. Cookham also had been unable to come to Frances's assistance, because it was his day for going into Newelbury to return the library books that he had finished during the weekend and to lay in a supply for the coming week. Both the Cookhams lived lives of rigid routine, which was a great support to them in their old age, and Catherine had long ago realised that it was a real unkindness to them to try to persuade them to vary any of their little rituals.

For herself, she enjoyed the strawberry picking. The fruit was so beautiful. Each plant was like a little mound of jewels. The smooth green leaves and the shining berries made designs so perfect that it seemed a desecration to disturb them. The fragrance of the fresh-picked fruit was tempting and heady.

A female blackbird kept hopping close to her feet, watching for grubs to carry home to the nest. Driven by the needs of her young, the bird was fearless. Indeed,

Drowned Rat

there was something almost companionable about her, as if she and Catherine were employed in a joint effort. Catherine wished that there were more days like this, when there was pleasant work to be done and the air was full of soft summer scents and the blueness of the empty sky drowned any worries that tried to come nagging at her mind.

Drowned them, did it? Why think of drowning? No one had drowned.

Yet it took the sight of her friend the blackbird joyously discovering a particularly succulent worm and flying away with it in triumph to make her forget that moment of uneasiness.

Presently Frances emerged from the house, carefully pushing a tea-trolley over the uneven ground. She pushed it into the shade of a gnarled old apple tree and brought chairs from the house and arranged them round the trolley.

"Break for lunch," she called out. "Come along. After lunch we'll try those roadside sales I was talking about. You two can go on picking and I'll see what sort of saleswoman I am. Not that cars wouldn't be much more likely to stop if they saw you two lovelies out there, but I can't take your place picking. My dears, you don't know how grateful I am to you both for helping me like this. I hope you enjoy your lunch. I've done my best. The labourer is worthy of his hire."

She flicked away the napkin with which she had covered the food on the trolley.

There was a jug of farm cider, pleasantly chilled. There was jellied consommé that had certainly not come out of a tin. There was fresh salmon mousse with a cucumber salad. There were long-stemmed glasses of zabaglione.

It was one of Frances's more surprising qualities that

she was a cook of great skill and although to enjoy the food that she provided it was best not to look into her kitchen and to start wondering how long it was that the odd bowls of unrecognisable and oddly smelling remnants had been left standing about, and when her stove had last been cleaned and the sink washed out, the food that emerged from the unappetising chaos was always excellent.

The dogs had followed her out and lay at her feet, panting in the heat. She ate heartily, but expected her guests to eat even more than she did. When the trolley had been cleared, Elspeth leant back in her chair, massaged her flat stomach and said, "I don't know how you expect me to do any more bending double over your strawberries after that."

"There's no hurry," Frances said. "Have a nice rest till you feel like getting started again. But I think I'll get our roadside stall set up. We've picked plenty to make it worth while to start selling. But I want to put some baskets aside for Irene and Andie and Nick. Are you going to see Nick later today, Elspeth? If so, you could take a basket to him."

Elspeth stretched and yawned. "I hadn't thought about it. He's working so hard at the moment, he hasn't much time for me. But I suppose I could pop in for a few minutes without disturbing him."

She did not sound enthusiastic.

"All right then, I'll get organised," Frances said. "Perhaps one of you would help me carry the table to the gate. I can manage the rest by myself."

She wheeled the trolley back to the kitchen.

Catherine followed her and a few minutes later the two of them came out again, carrying the kitchen table between them. By then Elspeth had sunk into a quiet doze.

Drowned Rat

Catherine and Frances carried the table to the gate, found a flat space where it would stand without wobbling, and while Catherine returned to the strawberry bed to go on picking, Frances arranged some rows of baskets on the table, got out some felt-tipped pens and an odd piece of cardboard, and in a few minutes had produced a quite decorative poster, giving the price of the strawberries and stating that they were fresh-gathered. Then she fetched a chair, her cigarettes and the dogs and settled behind the table to wait for the first car to stop. Elspeth roused herself dreamily and joined Catherine at the picking.

Neither of them went to the gate to see how Frances was faring, but from the strawberry bed they could see that trade was quite brisk, although spasmodic. Twenty minutes might pass without a single car stopping, then all of a sudden there would be a queue of three or four. Some of the people who stopped were friends of Frances's, who stayed chatting for several minutes. Others were people whom she had never seen before, but whom she somehow enticed into quite lengthy conversations. It was obvious that she was having a very happy afternoon. From time to time she left her station at the gate to demand new supplies.

"Haven't enjoyed myself so much for ages," she said on one of these occasions. "I realise I've wasted my life. I was born to be a saleswoman. They can't resist me. But don't let me get carried away and go and sell the lot. I do want to put some aside for Irene and the rest of you. What d'you think, mightn't it be best to do that now before supplies get too low? Choose some specially nice baskets and put them in the shade with some leaves over them, then we can take them round to everybody when trade begins to fall off. . . . Oh, there are some more customers."

She bustled back to the gate.

Catherine and Elspeth did as Frances had instructed, putting a number of baskets in the shade of the tree under which they had eaten their lunch, then going back to the picking. The work was drawing to an end. Only a few strawberries were left and those were mostly small ones, of the kind suitable only for jam. Frances had told Catherine and Elspeth to leave those, as she intended to have a jam-making orgy in a few days' time. Standing upright, Catherine called out to Elspeth that she thought it was time to stop.

Each of them had a few filled punnets to take to Frances at the gate. Carrying them there, they found her in conversation with Walter Hunnicut. He was squatting on the grass verge beside the gate, fondling one of the dogs, smoking one of Frances's cigarettes and eating his way through a basket of strawberries. He got quickly to his feet as the two girls appeared.

"Good afternoon, Miss Gifford," he said. "And Miss Wilde. I'd have come along to help too if I'd realised there was any shortage of labour."

"We've managed quite well, thank you," Catherine said. She put the baskets that she was carrying on the table. "This is just about the lot, Frances. We've only left the little ones, as you told us."

"Bless you both," Frances said. "If there's a thing I can't bear, it's waste. If I'd had to look on, seeing this glorious crop rotting into the ground, not to mention getting eaten up by birds or slugs, it would have broken my heart. Elspeth, Mr. Hunnicut tells me he's been up to Havershaw this afternoon to visit Douglas, but that he isn't there."

"Isn't he?" Elspeth said. "I didn't see him myself this

morning, but I got up earlier than I usually do because I was coming here, and I had breakfast by myself."

"You can't by any chance tell me where he's gone or when he'll be back?" the Australian asked.

"I'm sorry, I haven't the faintest idea," Elspeth answered.

"But he's home from the hospital, isn't he?"

"Oh yes, he got home yesterday afternoon."

"Quite well again, I hope." The grey eyes between his straw-coloured lashes were studying her intently while his wide mouth smiled.

"He didn't seem to have a thing the matter with him," Elspeth said. "Frances, if you want to send some of these strawberries to Nick, I could wander along with them now, if you like. Shall I do that?"

"Oh yes, dearie, that would be splendid," Frances said, "and you could take a basket for Irene too, couldn't you? I was thinking of shutting up shop here anyhow, if one of you will help me carry the table indoors. I'm getting a bit tired of sitting here and I feel like a little walk. Catherine, what about coming along with me to Andie's house, to take him his share? Then you could pick up your own on the way back."

"If you don't mind, I think I'll just go home," Catherine answered. Remembering the scene between Andie and Douglas the evening before, she had a reluctance to see either of them just then. "I've a lot of odds and ends I want to do."

"All right then, I'll go along to Andie's on my own," Frances said. "If you'll just help me with the table . . ."

"Let me," Walter Hunnicut said, and as Catherine and Elspeth picked up the remaining baskets, he lifted the table by himself, turned it upside down, balanced it on his head and said, "Where to?"

"Oh, how very good of you," Frances said. "I never meant to suggest . . . We could easily have managed it."

"A pleasure," he said. "Just show me the way."

Frances gave the little girlish skip that she often did when she was feeling unusually pleased and set off in the direction of the kitchen.

Catherine noticed how easily the small man walked with the weight of the table on his head. His stringiness, she thought, must be all muscle. He walked lightly behind Frances with neat, brisk strides, and it was only when he reached the kitchen that he faltered. He had not been prepared for what he found, walls painted all over with the ubiquitous ivy that Frances loved, a refrigerator decorated with trailing vines and massive bunches of purple grapes, pink, starry flowers painted all over the electric cooker, a stench of stale fat and of dog and of an unemptied plastic dustbin, and, circling everywhere, buzzing bluebottles.

But he faltered only for a moment. His observant eyes did not show his feelings. Lowering the table to the floor, he said, "Where do I put this?"

"Just where it is—that's perfect—and so very kind of you." Frances beamed at him, delighted with his attention. "Thank you so very much. And I must tell you how much I've enjoyed our little chat. I do so hope we can meet again while you're staying in Biddingfold. You'll come and see me, won't you, any time you feel like it? I'll show you the music Douglas used to play. So very advanced for his age. And some of those paintings of his I've got put away. Now, you will come and see me, won't you? Just drop in if you're passing."

Looking as if he could not get out of the kitchen quickly enough, Walter Hunnicut replied that he would be delighted to see her again, then backed out into the garden with a couple of hasty strides and, standing still for a moment, drew a very deep breath. Then he walked off to the gate while Frances stood in the doorway, waving at him.

"What a very nice man," she said when he had gone. "I do like Australians, they all seem so open and spontaneous. Do you think he really will drop in, or will he be too shy? If he is, I'll telephone and invite him. He was so interested in Douglas, you know, and what he was like when he was a boy. Now I'll just go over to Andie with his strawberries. A little walk will do me good. My back's never so bothersome if I make sure of taking a little regular exercise. And thank you again, dearies, for all your help. You've been wonderful. Help yourselves to all the strawberries you want, won't you?"

The party broke up, Elspeth walking towards the village to visit Nick, Frances turning into the lane to take the path to Andie's cottage and Catherine going on to her home.

At the gate she found Walter Hunnicut.

"I just wanted to ask you," he said, "did I offend the old lady by the way I bolted? I wouldn't want to do that. But that place took me aback."

"I thought you controlled yourself very well, considering," Catherine answered. "Of course, we're all used to it here, so we hardly give it a thought."

"There's nothing about her to give you any warning, is there?" he went on. "She seems so absolutely sane and normal."

"She's probably just as sane and normal as you or I," Catherine said, "except that she isn't as afraid as most of us are of enjoying herself in her own way. I rather wish I'd the courage to do the same."

"If you don't mind my saying so, I doubt if it's courage

you're short of," he said, "it's experience. You aren't cautious with people. As you know, I've been doing some inquiring round the place and none of you seems to have asked yourselves any questions about what kind of man Douglas Cable really is. You've just taken him at his own valuation."

"And why not?" she said. "Isn't it how we've taken you?"

"I don't think you have," he said. "I think you're pretty curious about me. Rightly, of course."

"Well, how would you like to come in for a drink now?"

"What I'd really like is another short talk with you."

"By all means. Come in."

She led the way into the house.

In the living room he roamed about restlessly while she was pouring out drinks for them both, and even when she had given him his and had sat down, he stayed standing in the middle of the room, looking uncertainly round him as if he were not quite sure what had brought him in.

Suddenly he said, "I'm leaving."

"Leaving Biddingfold?" Catherine asked.

"Yes."

"And going to London?"

"Going home. I can't do any good here."

"What good did you expect to do?"

"That's what I wonder now," he replied. "How could I think I could do anything?"

"I wish I knew what you wanted to do," she said.

"I wanted to track down a murderer. I thought I had evidence. I thought I might be able to stir things up so that something would come to the surface. But what do I find? While I've been hanging around, getting nowhere, someone else has been trying to murder the very man I've been after. So I've been thinking, whyever didn't I think of that myself? Take the law into my own hands—the law that won't touch him? But now I've thought of that, I'm clearing out, because one day I might find myself doing just that very thing, and even if they don't hang me, I don't want to spend the rest of my life in gaol."

Catherine came to her feet.

"Perhaps you don't want to be a murderer, but you don't mind being a slanderer, do you, Mr. Hunnicut?" she said. "Ever since you came here you've been spreading slanderous rumours about Douglas Cable. What have you really got against him?"

"It probably wouldn't do much good if I told you," he said. "But don't believe all he tells you about himself. You particularly. I like you. I trust you. I don't want you to be a victim. And you're just the kind he picks out—"

"I won't listen to this!" Catherine turned sharply to the door. "I think you'd better go—"

She was interrupted by the ringing of the doorbell.

It was rung several times in excitable succession, each ring longer than the one before it as if the desperation to be let in of whoever was out there was mounting uncontrollably. Then whoever it was simply kept a finger on the bell so that the shrill peal of it went on and on ringing through the house.

Catherine went running to the door. As she reached it she heard Frances outside crying sobbingly, "Catherine—Catherine, oh, come quickly! Catherine!"

Catherine opened the door.

Frances was on the doorstep. She was drenched with water. It plastered her hair to her head and ran in trickles down her broad face. Her sodden cotton dress clung to the soft bulges of her body and dripped on to the ground. The canvas shoes that she was wearing were both puddles of water.

"Oh God, I didn't know what to do, I could only think of coming here," she gasped. "Please come at once. He's in the pool, Catherine. I think he's dead. I went in as soon as I saw him and tried to get him out, but I'm seventy, Catherine, I'm so useless." Tears mingled with the water dripping from her hair. "I'm *sure* he's dead. His eyes were open under the water and he felt so stiff and strange."

Walter Hunnicut had followed Catherine to the door.

"In the pool, did you say? Show me the way and we'll see what we can do between us."

He went striding to the gate.

Catherine went running after him. Behind him, sobbing and panting, Frances followed. They reached the road, turned into the lane and started up the field path towards Havershaw.

Walter Hunnicut reached the pool well ahead of Catherine. She was just in time to see him plunge into it, as a few days before she had seen Andie dive in, and go swimming across it towards the figure sunk under the water just below the diving board.

A figure not in swimming trunks this time, but in a shirt, trousers and sandals. All the same, Catherine felt the horror of repetition about it, of losing her way in time because it had all happened before. Limp hair waved softly like weed around the sunken head, just as it had before. Only this time there was no question about it, this was death.

But it was not Douglas, it was Andie.

CHAPTER SEVEN

It was just as it had been on Friday evening, except that it was darker and the shadows of the chestnuts seemed to have taken a few strides forward, to stand more closely around them, and Andie was not as heavy as Douglas.

When Catherine took hold of him under the arms to help Walter Hunnicut lift him over the pool's edge, the dead body felt strangely light and fragile, as if it were all of thin, delicate bones, like a bird's. It did not embrace her, as Douglas had. It was too rigid. The blue eyes looked filmed, yet stared with a strange, accusing severity.

For a moment the only sound was the wheezing of Frances's breath. She had followed the other two too quickly up the path to the pool and had a hand pressed to her side, as if she were in pain there.

Then Walter Hunnicut climbed out of the pool and the sound of his splashing was added to Frances's panting.

Dripping water on to the paving, he said, "Now we get the police. It's a bit late for a doctor."

"I'll go," Catherine said, and, as she had on Friday evening, ran up the path to Havershaw to the telephone there, leaving Frances and Walter Hunnicut each standing a pace or two away from the dead man, silently looking down at him.

Catherine found Irene on the terrace, reclining in a long wicker chair. A book which it had become too dark for her to read was lying face down on her lap. She was wearing one of her frilly dresses and, without moving, was watching Catherine's hurried approach across the lawn.

Irene greeted her with a sigh. "I really must get glasses. I couldn't think who you were till you got quite near. I suppose you don't know where Elspeth is. I haven't seen her all day."

"I think she's with Nick at the moment," Catherine said. "She was with Frances before, helping her pick her strawberries. Irene, I've got to telephone the police. It's Andie. He was in the pool—drowned." Her voice was shaky. The short run up from the pool had made her pant as much as Frances.

"Andie!" Irene gave a little shriek and floundered up from her chair. Her book fell on to the grass. "You don't mean *drowned*—not dead!"

"Yes, dead, and I want to phone the police and I must talk to Douglas. Where is he?"

"I haven't seen him all day either. I haven't seen anyone all day."

"I must telephone, Irene."

"Yes, yes, of course. Come along."

Irene went striding along the terrace towards the glass doors that led into the little sitting room from which Catherine had telephoned before.

She hardly knew what she was doing when she telephoned Brian before the police. After all, wasn't a doctor the first person you needed? How could someone like herself, or Frances, or Walter Hunnicut, really judge of death?

Brian told her to telephone the police immediately.

She did so, then sat down and began to cry. If she had never succeeded in loving Andie with her whole heart, he had filled a considerable part of it for some time and the thought of his death was a tearing pain.

But the tears dried abruptly when Irene came loping past her with a cardigan on over her floating dress, saying, "We'd better go down to the pool, I suppose. But I do wish I knew what on earth has happened to Douglas. His car's out in front of the garage—the Rolls—but the Lotus isn't there. Why people can't tell one what they mean to do . . . He's going to be terribly upset about this, he was so fond of Andie. But how can we get in touch with him to tell him? If only he'd left a note or something. After all, it only takes a little thought to be considerate. . . . I could ring his club in London, I suppose, but he really loathes the place, you know, he hardly ever goes there. . . ."

She chattered on as she and Catherine went down to the pool, where nothing had changed. Only the shadows of the chestnuts had become a little darker and there was an evening hush in the air because no birds were singing.

Frances was sitting on one of the chairs by the poolside, with her head in her hands, clasping her wet straggle of hair and covering her eyes. Walter Hunnicut was standing just where he had been when Catherine had left them, as if in a self-appointed sentry duty, water dripping from his clothes on to the paving.

Later, in the confusion that followed when the police arrived, and the ambulance, and men with cameras and flashbulbs that gouged great gashes of light into the dusk, the three women and the Australian made their way up to Havershaw.

Catherine remembered that at some point Walter Hunnicut had said, "Seems as if someone around here doesn't like Australians."

But then Brian had come and it had felt natural that he should take her in his arms and hold her close.

"Your face," he said. "Don't look like that. It wasn't your fault, whatever he said."

Leaning her head against his shoulder, feeling his hands warm and firm on her, she found herself wanting to cry again. She stopped it by trying to concentrate on what he had said. He moved one of his hands and stroked her hair back from her forehead. It occurred to her as strange that this had never happened before, when they had known each other so well and for so long and she had so often wanted just such tenderness from him.

"What d'you mean—whatever he said?" she asked. "How could he say anything?"

"He left a letter," he said. "In the cottage. Not in an envelope, just lying on the table. I went there with Sturrock and we've both read it. He'll show it to you, of course, when you want to see it. But the thing I want to be sure of is that you don't start blaming yourself for anything. The man was blind drunk when he wrote it."

Catherine drew away from him and looked into his face.

"You're telling me Andie committed suicide and did it because of me," she said.

"That's more or less what his letter says," Brian answered. "I thought I might as well prepare you for it."

"And was he drunk?"

"We'll know more about that after the post mortem. But there are several empty whisky bottles lying around in his room and the place smells like a still and he seems to have had a hate session with those little sculptures of his. He did murder on nearly all of them with a hammer. They're lying around the room in splinters. And he went into the pool fully dressed, so it doesn't look as if he was meaning just to have a swim to cool off. And there's this letter . . ."

They had moved apart from one another and Catherine had sat down in a straight-backed Regency chair near the telephone. Walter Hunnicut also was in the room with her and Brian, but he had no reality for her. He had the ability to stand as completely still as if he were part of the furnishing, making as little claim on anyone's attention.

He was in the doorway to the garden now, looking out across the lawn to where lights still occasionally flashed through the trees. If he had spoken, it would have startled Catherine as much as if one of the long, proud Cable faces in some picture on the wall had suddenly addressed her. Irene had taken Frances upstairs to find some dry clothes.

"I want to see the letter," Catherine said.

"Of course," Brian answered. "But if I were you, I'd let Sturrock bring it when he's ready. He's been on to Newelbury and Chase is coming over. Superintendent Chase. There's something in the letter that—well, it looked as if it ought to be acted on at once. I'm not sure if I ought to tell you about it or not, but you'll hear about it soon anyway. And when you do see the letter . . ."

He made one of his pauses, so long that Catherine cried out, "What is it, Brian? Go on, go on!"

"You see, Andie confesses in it that he murdered Douglas," he answered.

In the doorway Walter Hunnicut turned his head and fixed his hard grey eyes on Brian's face. Then he looked with a detached kind of curiosity at Catherine, as if he were wondering how she would take this information.

She was aware of these slight movements, in fact all of a sudden was filled with an unreasoning dread of the small figure that could stand so still, outlined against the darkening evening sky.

"Do you know anything about this, Mr. Hunnicut?" she demanded in a voice that startled her by its shrillness.

"I expect I know less about it than you do, Miss Gifford," he said. "But I've been thinking. Manson was a fine swimmer, wasn't he?"

"Very."

"Well, d'you know how difficult it would be for a good swimmer to drown himself in a pool that size? It would be about as difficult a way of committing suicide as any he could choose. It would be different if he could swim straight out to sea and go on until he got too tired to turn back, or if he was caught in a storm, or rapids in a river. But even dead drunk, I think Manson would just have found that he couldn't help floating in that little pool."

"You mean, unless someone forced him under," Brian said.

"I heard him say, when he hauled Douglas out," Catherine said, "that you could drown yourself in a bucket of water if you gave your mind to it."

"Well, it was just a thought," Walter Hunnicut said.

"Brian, what do you think?" Catherine asked. "Did someone give Andie a blow on the head, like Douglas?"

"I haven't had much chance to find out," Brian said. "Tom Farquahar's coming over with Chase, and as there's no question that Andie's dead, I'd better not interfere before Tom gets here."

Tom Farquahar was the police surgeon in Newelbury.

"But you're sure Andie said he murdered Douglas," Catherine said, amazed and stunned.

"Yes."

"And Douglas has been missing all day."

"So Irene says."

"In the Lotus?"

"It's gone, anyway."

Catherine gave an abrupt shiver, feeling as if a breath from the last winter, or the coming one, had stroked her skin.

"It can't be true," she said. "They were such friends."

She chose to blot out from her mind the quarrel that had started in her own house the evening before. It had been, after all, a very small quarrel, which had ended almost as soon as it had begun.

"This Manson," Walter Hunnicut said, "was he a heavy drinker? That's something I was told about him in the village."

"Sometimes," Catherine said.

"Could he have been the one who hit Cable on the head on Friday? I mean, whatever he did today, or last night, or whenever it was, could it have been a second attempt?"

Catherine shook her head. "He was with me on Friday. We walked up here together from my house. And when he saw Douglas in the water, he was in like a streak of lightning to get him out."

"And Cable had only been knocked out for a few minutes, isn't that correct?" the Australian went on.

"Yes, or he'd have drowned, like Andie," Brian said.

"Then can you tell me this?" Walter Hunnicut said. "How is it no one saw Manson in the pool till Miss Knox found him there this evening? He'd been dead some time, hadn't he? Rigor was well advanced. Yet no one seems to have been to the pool all day, or along the path that skirts it, till Miss Knox went along it with her strawberries, or there'd have been an alarm raised about it hours ago."

Brian wrinkled his forehead as he studied the small man's questioning face.

"It's an interesting point," he said. "If the police don't raise it themselves, I'll point it out to them. I can't answer it myself. I don't even know how long ago Manson died. His having been immersed in cold water for we don't know how many hours isn't going to help anyone make an estimate."

"For instance," Walter Hunnicut said, "I believe Miss Wilde spent a good deal of the day helping Miss Knox pick her strawberries. And the shortest way from this house to Miss Knox's is by that path past the pool. So was Manson not in the pool yet when Miss Wilde went by, or did she just happen not to glance in that direction?"

"That's worth finding out," Brian said. "And we ought to find out if Irene simply decided not to have a swim today, for reasons of her own, or took a dislike to the idea of sharing the pool with a corpse."

"I'm not joking," Walter Hunnicut said.

"I'm sorry, neither am I," Brian said. "I merely mean it's obvious you're right—the actions of everybody will have to be checked, including the gardeners. Where were they all day? Speaking for myself, I haven't been near Havershaw today till I was sent for this evening. I expect I could prove that by checking over my appointments today. Catherine, what about you?"

"When I finished at the surgery I went home, changed and went straight to help Frances pick her strawberries," she answered. "And I spent the rest of the day there till she came rushing along to say she'd found Andie in the pool. That's to say, I'd just gone home and was having a talk with Mr. Hunnicut when she came back. And what about you, Mr. Hunnicut? When we found you talking to Miss Knox by the roadside in the afternoon, where had you come from?"

"From the village," he said.

"What brought you?"

"You'll remember I told you I wanted to have a talk with you," he said. "Naturally when I found you were busy, I waited till you were free."

"You waited just to tell me you'd decided to leave?"

"Right," he said.

"Although you still hadn't seen Douglas Cable."

She saw a sultry glow of anger in his pale eyes.

"Are you suggesting it was because I knew it wasn't any use waiting any longer—that I was leaving because I knew he'd been killed?"

"We don't know for sure that he has been killed," Brian said. "We've only Andie's word for it, and Andie was dead drunk."

"He may only have got drunk after he'd killed Cable and disposed of him," Walter Hunnicut said. "Isn't that probably how it happened? I'd say it was after he'd done the murder that he got drunk and sodden with remorse and killed himself—if he did kill himself, about which, as I told you, I have doubts. I think he may have got as far as trying to do it, and then, when he really wasn't in control of himself, had the job finished off for him."

"By the same person who knocked Douglas into the pool?"

"Why not?"

Catherine saw Brian studying the other man, so obviously measuring him for the part of murderer that he could not have failed to see it.

He gave a sardonic smile.

"Oh, I make a fine suspect," he said. "You could hardly do better than pick on me. And I can tell you a few things about this character who goes about knocking people on the head which may not have occurred to you. I almost feel as if I know him. He's an opportunist. He doesn't lay his plans in advance. There are two or three people he wants to eliminate—for all we know, we haven't got to the end of his list yet—and when he comes on them in some vulnerable situation he acts fast and then he gets out. And the way he chooses to act wouldn't need a great deal of strength. Take a man unawares, not dreaming of danger, with a pool there deep enough for him to drown in, I shouldn't say, for instance, it was beyond a woman to do it. Even though Cable and Manson were both big men."

"I'll tell you one thing," Brian said. "Yesterday evening about ten o'clock I passed the lodge. I thought of dropping in on Andie. I sometimes used to do that. We'd talk till late at night. He seemed a different person then from what he did when you met him round about—less truculent, less given to brooding on his grievances. He talked a lot about his work and showed me a good deal of how he set about it. I used to enjoy those talks. But last night when I got out of my car and went up to the lodge gates I heard voices shouting. I recognised them easily, they were Douglas and Andie. And there was a hell of a storm raging and I heard glass being broken. It's easy to say now I ought to have gone in and put a stop to it. I wish to God I had. But at the time I only thought this was the sort of situation where a stranger wasn't wanted. I hung about for a few minutes till I heard Douglas trying to talk reasonably, or that's how it sounded, and I thought he'd got things under control and knew how to handle Andie. So I didn't interfere, but got back in my car and went home."

He paused. He was gazing out through the door into the deepening darkness of the garden, where a group of figures, merging shadowily into one another as they moved, had begun to cross the lawn from the trees towards the house.

"And it's only just this moment that an odd thing's struck me," he said. "The Lotus wasn't there outside the lodge. Douglas must have walked there with Andie. And if Andie got rid of him in the Lotus, they must either have walked up to the house together to get it, in which case Andie didn't kill him in the lodge, or else he must have taken Douglas's keys after he'd killed him and come up to the house to fetch the car. He may have thought first he'd take the Rolls. Otherwise I don't know what it's doing in the drive. But he may have thought it would be too conspicuous. If it all happened in the night or perhaps the early morning, I suppose he'd a good chance of doing it without anyone hearing. But what a thing to do—to save a man's life one day and kill him three days later."

"Miss Gifford?"

A tall man stepped forward from the twilit garden into the light that fell on the terrace from the open door. He blinked slightly in the light. He was a thickset man with a round head and heavy shoulders. He moved with deliberation. His face had a high, fresh colour and he had round, rather protuberant eyes. He might have been a farmer except that he carried an air of authority that belonged in some way to the handling of human beings, and troublesome ones at that, rather than mild-tempered beasts.

Brian introduced him. "Superintendent Chase. Miss Gifford. And this is Mr. Hunnicut, a visitor from Australia."

"Australia?" Mr. Chase said. His lips were tight and looked unaccustomed to smiling. "A friend of Mr. Cable's then. You're staying in the house?"

"No, at the Green Man," Walter Hunnicut replied. "And I'm not sufficiently acquainted with Mr. Cable to call him a friend. I'm here this evening more or less by chance."

"He got Andie Manson out of the pool," Brian said.

"Ah, good, good," the superintendent said. "Glad to meet you, Mr. Hunnicut. I'd like a talk with you presently. But now I'd like a few words with Miss Gifford. There's this letter, for one thing, Miss Gifford, that you ought to see. We hope perhaps you can explain certain things in it to us."

Irene came into the room, followed by Frances, who was wearing mules of gilded leather and a silk dressing-gown brightly printed in crimson and gold, which plainly belonged to Irene, since it was much too long for Frances and was held up by a tightly tied belt at her waist. It gave her dumpy figure a rather regal air.

"Come into the drawing room, Mr. Chase," Irene said. "There isn't room for everyone in here. But first I simply must ring my daughter. I believe she's with Mr. Redmayne. I must tell her what's happened and get the two of them to come here. Don't you think I ought to do that? And I must find some dry clothes for Mr. Hunnicut. Come along, Mr. Hunnicut, I'll find you something of Douglas's."

"Don't trouble, I'm all right," he answered.

"Then come this way, please."

Irene swept them out of the room and along the passage to the room at the end of it.

It was a vast room with three tall windows that reached from the floor to the ceiling. They all looked out over the terrace and the lawns and now showed up as rectangles of greenish dusk against the white panelling of the walls. The ceiling was moulded with a pattern of delicate plaster wreaths. The fireplace, recently acquired by

Douglas, was genuine Adam, gracious and intricately carved.

It had amused Douglas to furnish the room with extreme formality. There was very little in it. There was an Aubusson carpet in soft and delicate colours. The stiff chairs and sofa, upholstered in pale grey velvet, were gilded and none of them comfortable. A *bonheur du jour* with beautiful marquetry stood between two of the windows. A great chandelier, a positive rain-storm of flashing crystal, hung from the centre of the ceiling. When Irene switched on the lights inside it everything in the room sparkled and shone, as if sunshine had suddenly broken through dark clouds and was striking irridescent lustre from every pendulous raindrop. Yet no room could have looked less welcoming, less inhabited.

"Just make yourselves comfortable," Irene said as Superintendent Chase and the others trooped into the room after her. She ran to the windows to draw the curtains of soft yellow brocade. "I'll ask Mrs. Forsyth to make you some tea. And perhaps you'd like some sandwiches. No, no, it's no trouble at all. Tea? Sandwiches? Yes, yes."

Without waiting to hear Mr. Chase say that he and his men required nothing, she darted out of the room.

In their stiff blue uniforms, the policemen who had followed the superintendent into the room could not have looked more incongruous amongst the gilding and the glitter and the soft, lovely, faded colours. Mr. Chase was not in uniform. He was in a suit of charcoal grey that looked a little too tight for him, as if he had recently been putting on weight. The room seemed to disturb him, as if he could not decide on which of the fragile chairs to sit down.

"Do you want to speak to Miss Gifford alone, or shall we come in?" Brian asked him from the doorway.

"Come in, come in," Mr. Chase answered. "D'you know, I haven't been in this room since old Mrs. Cable died? Solid Victorian it was in those days. All knickknacks and antimacassars and potted plants. But you wouldn't have been afraid of putting your feet up on the settee, if you know what I mean. Not that you'd have thought of doing that while Mrs. Cable was there. She liked dignity and good manners. But she always asked you in for a chat if you came collecting for a police charity, or anything like that. I can remember that happening when I was only twenty or thereabouts. It was one of the first jobs I had to do on my own and I was scared out of my wits. Not that she could have been friendlier, but there was something so grand about her. Of course, I got to know her well after a time and we used often to have a quiet joke together. Miss Gifford—" His tone changed abruptly. "Here's the letter. Take your time reading it, then tell us what it means to you."

He took a wallet out of his pocket, extracted something in a plastic envelope and handed it to her.

She found that she could read the letter through the plastic, yet she handled it gingerly, half afraid to touch it.

"Go ahead," he said encouragingly.

She nodded and began to read. The letter had been written in red, with a felt-tipped pen, in a writing that she recognised as Andie's, though she had never seen it so large and shaky before.

Catherine my darling love,

I've done it, I've killed him and that's a great load off my mind. What I've done I've done for you. When I saw you together I knew I should have to do it. He would have been able to do what he liked with you,

you wouldn't have stood a chance, and that wouldn't have been right. But I don't mean blame yourself, because you're as innocent as anyone I ever met. What I mean is, you never think evil of anyone. You took me as I was, you never wondered what I was really like, did you? But I know I'm no use to you, so all I can do for you is get rid of Doug before he does you any harm, and that's done now, over and done with, God be thanked I had the courage. I ought to have let him drown, then his death would be on someone else's conscience. But I still loved him myself then. I didn't understand the danger you were in. Good-bye, my dearest love,

Andie.

How many times Catherine read the letter she did not know. For what felt like minutes after she had read it through she went on staring at the sheet of paper behind its plastic shield until the words on it fused into a picture that had no special meaning. She had begun to shake, though this felt internal, and it did not occur to her that it showed until she felt Brian's hand on her shoulder, guiding her to one of the fragile gilded chairs.

"Some of that tea Irene promised wouldn't be a bad thing," he said.

Mr. Chase took the letter out of Catherine's fingers and put it back into his wallet.

"Miss Gifford, I'm going to ask you a personal question," he said. "Were you and Mr. Manson ever engaged to be married?"

She had dropped her head on to her hands and shook it faintly without answering.

"Was there anything else between you?"

"If you mean, were we lovers—no."

"Is there anything you can tell me about that letter?"

"Nothing much. Douglas Cable came to see me yesterday afternoon, mainly to thank me, I think, for having helped to get him out of the pool on Friday. And Andie Manson walked in and found us together. He seemed to get—upset about it. Jealous. I'd never realised before he was so jealous. He'd no reason to be. There was nothing between me and Douglas."

"Did Manson ever give you any presents?"

"Yes."

"Which you returned to him?"

She was startled. "No, oh no."

"You didn't?"

"No, why should I? We hadn't had any quarrel. And I love the thing, it's really beautiful, a little crouching man with such a wonderfully serene and peaceful face. And he never did anything I liked as much."

"Oh, one of his carvings."

"Yes, of course."

"I was talking about something else." He took a step towards her, holding out a hand. Cupped in it she saw a pair of opal ear-rings, oblong in shape, set in silver. "We found these in a drawer in his bedroom. I wondered if perhaps he'd given them to you and sometime you'd given them back."

A harsh cry, more like the bellow of an animal in the bush than a human sound, came from the throat of Walter Hunnicut, who was standing only just inside the doorway. Taking the detective by surprise, he pounced on the ear-rings, snatching them out of the superintendent's hand.

"Manson had these?" he yelled in the other man's face. "You said *Manson* had them?"

Mr. Chase mastered his surprise very quickly. But a shiny look of interest brightened in his protuberant eyes.

"Yes indeed," he said, "along with some cuff-links and socks and handkerchiefs and other odds and ends. They were the one item there which couldn't have belonged to a man and needed some explanation."

"The murdering rat, the bloody murdering rat!" Walter Hunnicut shouted. "And I thought all along it was Cable who killed her!"

CHAPTER EIGHT

Once he had hold of the ear-rings, they seemed to overpower him. He stood quite still, except that his small, stringy body had begun to tremble. He held the ear-rings close to his eyes, gazing at their greenish iridescence as if he were taking a long, deep look into the eyes of someone he loved. He whispered several words to himself which had the tone of an almost unbearable tenderness and for a moment his eyes filled with tears. Then he coughed loudly, looked round the room as if it surprised him to find anyone there besides himself, and held the ear-rings out to Mr. Chase.

"I'm sorry—you'll be wanting these as evidence," he said.

"That's right," Mr. Chase said. "But evidence of what, Mr. Hunnicut? It looks as if you've something to tell us. Do you wish to make a statement?"

"I'll tell you a story," Walter Hunnicut said, "if that's what you mean. And you can write it down if you want to and I'll sign it. And I don't mind who hears it, so there's no need for anyone to leave the room. You've all been speculating about me and wondering what I was up to, so you may as well hear the truth now. Someone may even be able to help."

He leant on the back of a chair, folding his arms on it in their wet shirt sleeves. His gaze went up to the glittering crystals of the great chandelier as if they were merely a screen of dancing water from a fountain between him and some scene that he could see quite clearly.

"I used to have a wife," he said. "June. I'd got a job too, working as a salesman for one of the wineries in South Australia. We'd a home in a place called Hawkwell—that's in the Barossa Valley, near Adelaide—just a village, you'd call it, I expect. Naturally I was away a good deal and June came from Sydney and enjoyed a bit of life and was dead bored in Hawkwell. But I always thought I'd get something better some day and maybe get into one of the cities and I never thought she was actually unhappy. We'd a daughter Coral—she's five now—and June seemed to think the world of her. And then one day she vanished. I was away on a trip and the first anyone knew anything was wrong was hearing Coral screaming in the house. No one knew how long she'd been shut up alone there, she didn't know herself. A neighbour took her in and because there wasn't a sign of June, got hold of the police to try to get a word to me. But I was on the move and it was a day or two before they caught up with me. I went straight home. There still wasn't a word of June and when I started going through her things, as the police wanted me to, I couldn't find anything missing. None of her better clothes, anyway, or any baggage. There was a cotton dress she used to wear a lot that I couldn't find, and some sandals, and those ear-rings you've got there. I gave them to her when we were first married and she used to wear them most of the time. Some people say opals are unlucky. That didn't worry her. She liked them. She said they went with nearly everything she wore."

He blinked and frowned up at the lights above him as if for a moment he found their shimmer distracting.

"I was dead scared from the first," he went on. "Not just that she'd left me but that something had happened to her. Whatever she did, and we'd had fights more than once over men she'd taken up with when I was away, she'd always taken good care of Coral. It just wasn't like her to go and leave the kid shut up in an empty house. God, if that neighbour hadn't heard her, the child could have died of starvation. So I was always sure from the start something had happened to June. And the police got hunting for her. But the only thing they turned up about her was that on a night a day or two after I'd left on my trip, she'd been seen in a pub with a feller called Doug Cable. He was a salesman like me for one of the wineries and we'd come across each other casually. As I've said to you people here, I'm not sure we'd ever exchanged a word. I knew him by sight, but that was all. I didn't even know he'd met June. But then people began to tell me they'd often seen him dropping in at the house when I was away. So I started to look for him. But he'd clean vanished; at least that's how it looked at first till I somehow heard he'd come into money and gone back to England, where he'd come from."

"And did you find your wife?" Mr. Chase asked so quietly that it sounded as if he did not want to interrupt the other man's flow of words.

"Not a trace of her," Walter Hunnicut answered. "It looked as if she'd gone out to do the shopping in her old cotton dress and sandals and simply walked off the face of the earth."

"Would she have left the child alone in the house if she'd gone to do the shopping?"

Walter Hunnicut withdrew his gaze from the hypnotic lights to give the superintendent a steady look.

"You're quick," he said. "No, she wouldn't."

"Would she have gone anywhere, leaving the child alone in the house?"

"No."

"So you think someone came to the house and forced her to go away with him, whether she wanted to or not."

"It's the likeliest thing."

"What about those times when she was seen in the pub? Would she always have fixed up a baby-sitter?"

"I think so. Our neighbour, Mrs. Barber, was a widow and a bit lonely, and she liked to come in and sit with the kid."

"How was the child dressed when she was found—pyjamas, frock or what?"

"You're thinking that might be a clue to when it happened. Well, she was stark naked."

"Was that usual?"

"Yes, it didn't mean much. She generally slept naked in the hot weather. And we'd a sort of little plastic bathing pool in the garden and she used to play about naked in that. And sometimes she'd run around the house without a stitch on. But the doors were found locked and the windows shut and our one air-conditioning unit was turned on, and June usually only switched it on for a time in the evening to cool our bedroom down for the night, because of what it costs to run, so it's a good guess he came after, say, eight o'clock."

"Does it get dark there pretty early?"

"Oh yes, much earlier than here."

"So it would have been easy for him to come and go without being seen."

Walter Hunnicut nodded. "Of course, the police in Hawkwell have been over all this. It was quite a famous disappearance case for a time. Our papers gave it a lot of coverage. And Scotland Yard investigated Cable for them. But he wouldn't have told you anything about that."

"No." Mr. Chase looked at the ear-rings in his hands,

which changed from green to fiery red as he moved them. "Has anything ever been heard about her? For instance, was a body discovered that could have been hers?"

"No."

"So it's possible she's alive and well somewhere."

"That's what our police ended up trying to make me believe."

"But you positively identify these ear-rings as hers."

"I do."

"Aren't they turned out like this in thousands?"

"No two opals are the same. And the settings are handmade. I'm ready to swear to them. And anyway, wouldn't it be a bit much of a coincidence if they weren't hers?"

Mr. Chase cocked his round head a little on one side. "You're remembering it was Mr. Manson's house they were found in, not Mr. Cable's? Had you ever met Mr. Manson before you came here?"

"No, and not after I came here either. I don't know anything about him."

"If your wife had been seeing him as well as Cable, you didn't know about it?"

"No."

"Or that he and Cable were apparently close friends before they came here?"

"I told you, I'd never heard of him."

"Yet a few minutes ago you called him a murdering rat, so now you think it may have been Mr. Manson who killed your wife, if anyone did, and not Mr. Cable."

Walter Hunnicut tilted his head back again to look deeply into the clustered lights overhead. He blinked at them several times, as if to clear his vision.

"He's admitted to killing Cable, hasn't he? And he'd got the ear-rings. And if he and Cable were close friends back home, June could quite easily have been seeing them both. I think I may perhaps have been doing Cable a wrong, particularly as no one here has a thing to say against him, whereas Manson's had them puzzled. Not a friendly man, they've said, and often sour-tempered, and sometimes violent if he'd been drinking too much. He didn't make himself much liked."

"That's because he's an artist," Catherine said defensively, feeling that the dead Andie had the right to some kind of loyalty from her. "You couldn't expect them to understand him."

She hoped somehow that Brian would support her, but he said nothing.

In the brief silence that followed, the door opened and Mrs. Forsyth appeared, pushing a tea-trolley.

There was tea on it and a plate of bulky sandwiches, of a size that she had probably thought suitable for policemen. As she withdrew Irene came in and started pouring out tea. Frances, on seeing the sandwiches, immediately helped herself to one, sat down on a sofa and began to eat.

"That's the stuff to give the troops," she said. "I'm famished. It's been a very tiring day. You know, Mr. Chase, I had a thought while I was upstairs and Mrs. Cable was finding these lovely clothes for me. The Lotus is missing, isn't it? And it probably has poor Mr. Cable's body inside it. Well, if poor Andie drove him off in it, dead or alive, it can't be far away, can it? I mean, because Andie must have been able to walk back from wherever he left it to drown himself in the pool. So you needn't look very far. And the kind of places you might look first are the old quarry at Olding, and the bridge beyond Brigham Farm, where they're always having accidents, and perhaps Lagham Lake. It's very easy to drive off the road there into quite deep water. I can remember several cases of it. Anyhow, I'm sure you needn't look further off than three or four miles. If Andie was really as drunk as they say, he won't have felt like walking far."

Mr. Chase's voice was full of patience. "As a matter of fact, we've already acted on that assumption, Miss Knox," he said. "We've men out searching now."

"Yes, of course—sorry, I didn't mean to try to teach you your job," Frances said. "But there's another thought I had I must tell you about. D'you think Andie Manson really wrote that letter you found? Could it possibly have been a forgery?"

"It's a question we shall take into consideration," Mr. Chase said. "We shall have it examined by experts. But have you any particular reason for making that suggestion, Miss Knox? Does it seem to you unlikely that Manson wrote that letter?"

"Oh no, not really," she said. "It's only that forgery's so extremely easy. I'm quite good at it myself. I found that out accidentally. I was doodling on the envelope of a letter I'd just received while I was thinking about how to answer it—I think it was a rather stiff reminder that I was to pay some bill or other—and I suddenly saw to my surprise that I'd written my own name and address in exactly the same handwriting as was on the envelope already. I was very amused and tried to do it again. It wasn't quite so successful the second time, but with a little practice I found I'd a remarkable knack of copying other people's handwriting. Of course, I never made any use of it, I just did it for my own entertainment. The fact is, you see, I'm quite clever with my hands. I'm not exactly what you could call artistic, but I do quite a lot of painting around the house and I think anyone who's trained himself to do that kind of thing could easily learn the trick of forgery."

"Have you anyone special in mind?" Mr. Chase asked. "Anyone specially artistic?"

"Well, of course, there was Andie himself—very artistic indeed. But he wouldn't have needed to forge his own writing, so we won't count him. And there was Mr. Cable, who was a very clever painter when he was a boy, but I don't think he kept it up, and the only reason I can think of why he might have wanted to forge a confession by Andie to his own murder is that he wanted to disappear. Do you think that's possible?"

The superintendent's eyes were developing a slightly glazed look as Frances's speech flowed rapidly on.

"Have you any reason for thinking Mr. Cable might want to disappear?" he asked.

"No, no, this is all hypothetical," Frances said. "It just happens that I've an extremely logical mind. I can't help it if I have to follow any chain of reasoning that occurs to me to its conclusion. But perhaps Mr. Cable would have wanted to disappear if Mr. Hunnicut's suspicions come anywhere near the truth. Or, of course, if he'd just murdered Andie. However, to resume, there's Mr. Redmayne, who's extremely clever at drawing maps. He does all the ones in those travel books of his, you know. He's an excellent draughtsman. And I'm sure there are lots of other people in the neighbourhood who could easily develop a talent for forgery if they gave their minds to it. Only I do understand you've no reason yet for thinking the letter *is* a forgery. As usual, I'm running ahead too fast. Do please forgive me."

The door was flung open. Elspeth came in with a little rush. Seeing so many people in the room, she halted, looking as if the lights dazzled her, then she ran to her mother and wound her arms round her neck.

"Mummy, it isn't true, is it, Douglas isn't dead?" she cried.

Nick followed her into the room. He and Mr. Chase appeared to have met before, for they only nodded briefly to one another. Standing still just inside the door with his shoulders hunched and his hands in his pockets, Nick had a sullen look in his heavy features and an air of having been brought there against his will, of waiting impatiently for the first opportunity to leave.

"We don't know, darling," Irene answered, holding Elspeth close to her. "Andie left a letter, saying he'd killed Douglas, and Douglas has been missing all day and so has the Lotus, but we don't really know what happened between them."

Elspeth's eyes filled with tears. She buried her face on her mother's shoulder.

"I don't think I can bear it," she said. "It can't have happened. Not to Douglas."

Irene stroked her hair. It occurred to Catherine that she had never really noticed before how close the mother and daughter were to one another, how much each depended on the other.

"Perhaps it hasn't," Irene said gently. "Perhaps it's all some kind of awful mistake."

"It's got to be," Elspeth said. "I think I'll die if it's true."

Without saying a word, but with a look of blazing fury on his face, Nick turned and walked out of the room.

"Just a moment, Mr. Redmayne," Mr. Chase called after him. "There's a question I'd like to put to you while you're here, and to all the rest of you before you go home. We don't know yet at what time Andrew Manson died, or exactly how, but we do know he was in that pool for a good while before he was found. . . ."

"Ah!" Walter Hunnicut interrupted.

Mr. Chase raised his eyebrows, waiting for him to continue.

"It's only that I know what you want to ask us," Walter Hunnicut said. "Just how did it come about that no one found Manson's body earlier in the day? I've been asking that question myself."

"And have you arrived at any answer?" Mr. Chase asked.

The small man shook his head. "I didn't find him myself because I didn't come to the house or the grounds till Miss Knox came to Miss Gifford's home, where I happened to be at the time, saying she'd found him in the pool."

"I didn't find him because I've been at home all day, working," Nick said. "Is that all you want with me? If it is, I'd like to get back now."

"Thank you, Mr. Redmayne, that's all."

Nick left the room again, without even a glance at Elspeth.

"Mrs. Cable?" Mr. Chase said.

"Well, I just didn't go down to the pool all day, although it was so warm," Irene answered. "I never care much for swimming by myself and my daughter was away, helping Miss Knox with her strawberries, and of course Mr. Cable was nowhere about. So I spent most of the day on the terrace, reading."

"Miss Gifford?"

"I went to my usual job at the surgery," Catherine answered, "then spent the rest of the day picking strawberries for Miss Knox."

"And you, Miss Knox—were you at home all day until you came up to the pool and found Mr. Manson?"

"Yes, Mr. Chase."

"Dr. Walsh?"

"I did my normal day's work, morning and afternoon surgeries, visited patients. I didn't come here till I was sent for."

"And Miss Wilde?"

Elspeth drew slightly away from her mother, tossed back her hair and brushed her eyes with the back of her hand.

"It was just chance I didn't find him," she said. "If it happened early, that is. Normally, when I got Miss Knox's telephone call, asking me to help her, I'd have gone down to her house by the path past the pool. But just as I was going my mother called out to me that she'd some letters she'd like me to post in the village. So I walked down the drive to the post-office, and that meant that the shortest way to Miss Knox's house was by the road. So I never went near the pool."

"But you passed the lodge," Mr. Chase said.

"Yes."

"About what time was that?"

"Oh, I suppose about half past nine."

"Did you notice anything unusual about it?"

"Unusual?"

"Well, for instance, was a door open that would normally have been shut, or did you happen to catch a glimpse of Mr. Manson or anyone else inside the cottage, or was Mr. Cable's Lotus at the gate?"

Elspeth gave her head a slow shake. "No, I can't think of anything. I definitely didn't see Andie and the Lotus wasn't there. I—I can't think of anything. I was thinking rather hard of something else, you see. You know I'm engaged to Mr. Redmayne. Well, I'd begun to wonder if that was a mistake and I was turning it over in my mind—"

"Elspeth!" her mother broke in. "Mr. Chase isn't the

least bit interested in your relations with Nick. They have nothing to do with this matter. And even if you and Nick have been quarrelling, I'm sure it doesn't mean a thing. He's got a very quick temper, everyone knows that, and if you love him you must just learn to put up with it."

"But I'm not sure if I do love him," Elspeth said. "I'm not sure if I love him enough. This ghastly thing that's happened to Douglas, it makes me realise—"

"Please!" Irene interrupted again. "We can talk about this later. Mr. Chase has other things on his mind. Mr. Chase, it's just occurred to me that you probably want to interview the gardeners. They're the most likely people to have been near the pool, though as a matter of fact I believe they were both working in the vegetable garden all day. They've gone home by now, of course, but Pearson lives at 12 Churchill Terrace—it's one of the new council houses—and Barkley lives at Laburnham Cottage, just behind the church."

"Thank you," Mr. Chase said. "But first I'd like to question the servants here, to find out when they last saw Mr. Cable."

Irene did not think the drawing room a suitable place for the questioning of servants and took the superintendent to the housekeeper's room.

Before he went out Brian asked, "Are you finished with us? Any objection to our going home now?"

"None at all, Dr. Walsh," Mr. Chase replied. "If anything further crops up I'll get in touch with you."

"Then I'll drive you home," Brian said to Catherine. He added to Frances, "I suppose you've got to wait here till your clothes are dry, so you won't be wanting a lift yet."

"That's right, dearie," Frances said. "I couldn't very well go off in this gorgeous garment of Irene's, could I?" She looked as if she rather liked the thought of herself in the gorgeous garment and was in no hurry to change. "But don't worry about me. I'll walk home as usual. I'm not afraid of the dark."

"Elspeth will drive you home when you want to go," Irene said. "Won't you, darling?"

Elspeth looked too buried in her woe to answer, then possibly because she realised that this would mean driving the Rolls, smiled sweetly and said, "Of course."

Catherine was not usually afraid of the dark, but that evening she was glad not to have to make her way home alone. But when she and Brian went to his car, they found it blocked by one of the police cars.

"Never mind, don't bother them about moving it," she said. "I'll walk."

"I'll come with you then," Brian said. "I don't think it's right for you to be out and about alone tonight. There might be ghosts walking."

"What do you mean?" she asked.

They started across the lawn towards the grove of chestnuts. The moon had risen and the grass was washed with silvery light, but the trees had an eerie look of leaning together to whisper secrets to one another.

"The ghosts we've all got tucked away at the backs of our minds," Brian said. "Anyway, I've got a good few myself. Most of the time they leave me in peace, but given the right circumstances they get out and walk."

"Oh yes, of course I've got some of them too," Catherine said. "But you're the last person I'd have thought of as being bothered by them."

"Don't you think we've both been suffering from rather a lot of delusions about one another?" He slid an arm round her shoulders, bringing her to a standstill. "Catherine, I love you very much. Do you know that, or have you simply never noticed?"

"I haven't noticed it, Brian," she answered. "You've never made it—very noticeable."

"That was because of Andie. Recently, that is. When I first came here you were so very, very young. Then your father died and I thought all I was to you was a shoulder to cry on. And then Andie came and ever since then I've just thought, what's the use? And then this evening I realised you weren't in love with him at all."

"Why this evening?"

"Because his death upset you, shocked you, grieved you, but it didn't tear you to pieces."

She gave a slight shiver as the memory came to her of the figure lying dark and still in the water, only a little way from where they were standing now.

"Poor Andie," she said.

"Even if he's a murderer?"

"He must have been mad when he did it. I know I never really understood him at all. I just realised he was very strange and unstable. Brian . . ." She moved closer into his arms. "When you first came here, didn't you realise I fell in love with you at once?"

"No, I didn't. Why should I? There seemed to be so many others around you at the time."

"I never cared for anyone after I'd met you."

"What a lot of time we've wasted then, haven't we?"

Their hold of one another tightened and the trees near them seemed to give up their secret whispering of sinister things and to stand peaceful and still.

Presently they walked on slowly, hand in hand. Catherine dreaded the moment when they would reach the pool and their mood would inevitably be shattered. But before they reached it Brian halted again and again kissed her and her fear of any ghosts that might lurk behind the trees faded. There was only the memory of Andie, never understood, never loved enough. Not a ghost.

"What a night for this to have happened to us," Brian said. "Three hundred and sixty-four other days in the year and we have to choose this one to come to our senses. Though perhaps the day chose us. But part of my mind's still on that policeman and the questions he asked us and the ones he didn't."

"I don't think either of us could stop thinking about that, however hard we tried," Catherine said. "And tonight isn't going to be the only night in our lives. What questions didn't he ask?"

"I was thinking about what Frances said about forgery. She suggested Douglas could have forged that suicide note because he suddenly wanted to disappear, either because he'd murdered Andie or because Hunnicut had tracked him down. But Chase didn't go into that at all. So has he already found Douglas's body? Does he know for a fact that Douglas is dead?"

"It's the likeliest thing, isn't it?"

She gave a sigh. A tune had begun to revolve in her brain, that most banal but catchy of tunes, naturally connected with Andie, Douglas and Walter Hunnicut, "Waltzing Matilda," the tune to which, she had been told, the Australians had gone to the war. She could not get it to stop. She tried to think clearly, but the low, humming sound that buzzed in her head confused her.

"We know the two of them had a quarrel," she said, "the one I heard the beginning of—"

She caught her breath sharply. The sound was not in her head. It was only her nervous exhaustion that had made her think so. The tune was coming from beside the pool and had just taken on words.

"'. . . And his ghost may be heard as it sings in the billabong,
Who'll come a-waltzing Matilda with me?'"
"Douglas!" she cried.
Brian strode forward. Catherine hurried beside him.
Douglas was sprawled comfortably in one of the chairs beside the pool. He had a cigarette in his hand. The tip of it glowed red in the deep shadows. He was smiling contentedly, as they saw when they were close enough to see his face fairly clearly in the darkness.

"D'you know the hardest thing in the world to get two Australians to agree about?" he said. "A definition of a billabong. Try asking them when you get the chance. Every single one of them will tell you something different."

CHAPTER NINE

"What *is* a billabong?" Catherine asked. In the circumstances it sounded ridiculous, but she could not think of anything else to say.

"Well, I can give you my definition." Douglas crossed one leg over the other, clasping his ankle in one hand. "But remember I'm not a dyed-in-the-wool Australian. I got there too late in life to become one. I'd say a billabong is a sort of backwater from a river that sometimes curves back into it and sometimes just fades out in the sand. That's all."

"You wouldn't say this pool is anything like a billabong?" Brian asked.

"Good God, no. You'd never think of swimming in one. For one thing, it'd be dried up a good deal of the time and even when there was water in it, it'd be full of rocks and roots of dead trees and altogether a very dangerous place for a bathe."

"This pool seems to be a fairly dangerous place for a bathe," Brian said.

Douglas was silent, looking steadily at him as if he sensed antagonism in him and wanted to discover the source of it.

"I was only singing, you know, because I wanted to draw your attention to the fact that I was here," he said. "I saw you coming and I didn't think you'd welcome an audience."

Drowned Rat

"But, God, man, don't you know what's happened?" Brian asked.

"I was just going to ask you, what *has* happened?" Douglas said. "I got to the lodge. I found police cars at the gates. I saw all the lights on in Andie's cottage. I saw more police cars in the drive up to the house. So I thought I'd drive on up the road, leave the car there and come this way to see if I could get in and find out quietly what's been going on. Then I heard the two of you coming and thought you'd prefer it if I drew your attention to my presence."

"It happens that you're supposed to be dead," Brian said. "That's part of what the police are investigating. And Andie *is* dead."

"*Andie* . . . ?" Douglas jerked forward in his chair. He looked quickly from Brian's face to Catherine's. In the moonlight all three were very pale. "What happened?"

"Well, he seems to have got himself dead drunk," Brian answered, "then sometime last night or early this morning he wrote a letter to Catherine telling her he'd murdered you, apparently because he was afraid she'd fall in love with you, then came here and drowned himself. His body was found by Frances Knox in the early evening."

"And that's all?"

"*All?*" Brian said. "Isn't that quite a lot to have happened?"

Douglas passed a hand over his face, pinching his features together, then let it go. It looked stiff and empty.

"Didn't he write anything about what happened between us last night?" he asked. "That's what I meant."

"No," Brian said. "But I was going to drop in on him yesterday evening, just for a chat, so I know the two of you had a flaming row. But I didn't think you'd want me walking in on you, so I left you to it."

"I wish to God you hadn't. If you'd come in, you might have known how to handle him. An injection or something. It's all my fault, of course. I thought it was all right to leave him. How wrong you can be!" Douglas got heavily to his feet. "He murdered me? He wrote he murdered *me* . . . ?" His tone was dazed. "The fool saved my life the other day, didn't he? I know we had that bloody stupid quarrel, but it didn't mean anything. That is, it didn't mean anything much to me. He's jealous—he *was* jealous as hell, of course, and he'd got it into his head, because he found us together, that there was something between Catherine and me. And when we got back to the lodge yesterday, when I thought I'd calmed him down, he started drinking heavily. Really heavily, I mean. He doesn't do it often, but when he does—did—oh damn, I can't get it into my head he's dead—when he did, it sometimes led to trouble. He got violent, you see. Once it landed him in gaol. Last night he started taking it out on his sculptures. I tried to stop him, but he went for them with a hammer, smashing them to splinters. Terrible thing to do, there were some lovely things amongst them. I managed to bundle a few of them away out of sight, but there weren't many left by the time he'd finished. He kept shouting at me too, telling me I was a fake to pretend I believed in him, and that I needn't worry, I shouldn't be bothered with him much longer. I never guessed what he meant. I thought he was just talking about going back to Australia and that he'd have forgotten it by the morning, and when he finally passed out I got him on to the couch and covered him with a blanket and left him, thinking he'd be all right. I suppose the truth was that he hadn't passed out at all, he was only putting on an act to get rid of me because he'd already decided what he meant to do.

But murder . . . Christ, man, why should he write to Catherine that he'd murdered me? I'm alive, aren't I?"

"If he was as drunk as you say, we don't know what he had in his mind," Brian said. "He may have passed out quite genuinely and when he came round not been able to remember what really happened, but only something about a fight, and seen the wreckage of his work all round him, and convinced himself he'd killed you and so come and drowned himself."

"Do you think that's how it was?"

"It could have been."

"And the police believed what he wrote and are looking for my corpse?"

"Yes, they're looking for your corpse."

"That's an irony, if you like!" Douglas gave a painful little laugh. "D'you know what I've been doing today? I went up to London because I felt I owed Andie something for saving my life. In spite of that quarrel. I told you, it didn't mean anything to me. There've been too many others like it. He'd be sheepish next day and say he was sorry and that'd be that. Well, I went up to London to buy Andie a present. Just a token, because I'd really something else in mind. I got him a watch, a nice one, gold, with a nice bracelet and a second hand, and it's waterproof and anti-magnetic and what have you. He really liked that sort of thing more than you'd expect. Here it is."

He put a hand in a pocket and brought out a narrow package. He started to tear the wrapping away with shaking fingers.

"He wasn't an easy sort of bloke to help, he'd such a damn lot of pride," he said. "But I thought this once he'd take a present in the way it was meant. And the thing I really went to London to do—that's why I was so late getting home—was go to see a man I know—not very well, but just enough to ring up and say I wanted to see him. He's the manager of the Gibbon Gallery and I've bought quite a few things there. So I thought I'd stick my neck out to see what I could do for Andie. And I got the feller to say he'd come down to Havershaw next weekend and talk to Andie and look at his stuff, what's left of it. I piled it on a bit, as I thought, about what a temperamental character he was and how he'd just destroyed a lot of his best stuff and how I thought something ought to be done for him before he went to pieces completely. . . ."

He had managed to unwrap the package and opened the slim leather case inside it. There was a very handsome watch there that shone softly in the moonlight on its satin cushion.

With a sudden loud curse he hurled it into the swimming pool.

"There you are, Andie!" he shouted. "It's yours! Take it, damn you! Take it to hell with you!"

A moment afterwards he collapsed in the chair in which he had been sitting before, took hold of his head in both hands and sat there, trembling all over.

Catherine stood waiting for Brian to say something or do something. She felt helpless herself, for if she were somehow to blunder, she thought, Douglas might lose all control of himself, perhaps even turning on her because in some way she had been at the bottom of what Andie had done.

She was astonished when she heard how coldly Brian spoke.

"You remember the other day we talked about a man called Hunnicut, Douglas?"

Douglas did not answer. He was still shaking. His face was hidden.

Brian went on, "He's up at Havershaw now—"

"For Christ's sake!" Douglas roared at him, throwing back his head. "Don't you understand, I've just lost my best friend. One of the only friends I've ever had. I don't count all you crowd who've come swarming around me here. Andie and I were mates when we hadn't a cent between us. Why else d'you think I looked after him when he followed me here? Why d'you think he *did* follow me, if he didn't know I'd share everything I had with him. A man called Hunnicut! Let me get my hands on him! I'll see he drowns in this pool!"

"The man in question," Brian said coolly, "is of the opinion that either you or Andie murdered his wife. He was fairly sure it was you until the police discovered some opal ear-rings in a drawer in the lodge which he swears were his wife's. So now he thinks the murderer may have been Andie. Whatever the facts are, I think you're going to have to face him sooner or later. Seeming to avoid him could give a bad impression."

A curious change came over Douglas's face. From being distorted with anger and grief, it twitched into a grin of sardonic amusement.

"I do believe you half believe this bloke," he said.

"I only think he'll have a lot of other people believing him if you don't do something about it," Brian said. "All of us who came swarming round you here—you yourself don't depend much on our friendship, do you?"

"Look, forget what I said about that, will you?" Douglas stood up and laid a hand on Brian's shoulder. "I didn't mean it. It's meant a lot to me, the way you've accepted me since I came home. I'm not myself just now. Can you wonder? This character Hunnicut, he's still up at the house, you say?"

"He was when we left," Brian answered.

"Then d'you feel like coming back with me to give me some moral support when I face him? I'd be glad if you'd just help me break it to Irene and the others that I'm back from the dead. I don't like to think of what I'll see on their faces. It might not be a welcome."

Brian looked questioningly at Catherine. Her own inclination was to go home. She was extremely tired and she longed to be alone with Brian. But she did not want to refuse Douglas. She nodded.

"Then we may as well get the car and drive up to the house," Douglas said, "or I'll have to come back for it sometime later."

They set off down the path towards Catherine's house.

The Lotus was at the end of the lane. The three of them got into it and Douglas drove to the gates of Havershaw. The lodge was now in darkness and all was quiet. Brian's car was there, beside the Rolls, but the police cars had gone.

Getting out of the Lotus, Douglas said, "Really, I'm curious to know how they'll look when I come back from the dead. The chances of doing that don't often come one's way. It'll be almost as good as being able to sit up and take a good look round one at one's own funeral."

He went ahead towards the steps that led up to the front door of the house, flung it open and walked swiftly along the wide passage to the open door of the brightly lit drawing room.

Frances was still there, still sitting on a sofa, dressed in crimson and gold and munching sandwiches. Irene, looking drained and feeble, was sitting with her head back against the pale grey velvet of one of the gilded chairs. Her long, slender hands clawed at the arms of the chair as if she could hardly bear to listen for a moment longer to the talk in the room. This was between Elspeth and

Walter Hunnicut. Elspeth was squatting on the carpet at her mother's feet with an arm across her knees and her head resting on it. Walter Hunnicut was standing, as he had been before, leaning on the high back of one of the chairs.

Elspeth was saying, "I'll tell you what I think, Mr. Hunnicut, I think she killed herself. I think you're probably right, she was madly in love with him and he didn't love her at all. And so, you see, she killed herself. And that may be why he wouldn't look at another woman ever since. He felt so terrible about it—felt, you know, that the same thing could happen all over again if he let himself care for anybody—"

It was at that moment that she saw Douglas in the doorway and gave a wild shriek.

Irene gave a little jerk in her chair and sat up. Apparently she had been asleep.

"Oh, for heaven's sake, Elspeth," she began irritably, then saw Douglas, caught her breath and was silent.

Frances smiled and with her mouth full said, "Dearie, how nice. But the funny thing is, you know, I've been expecting it. I'm sure if you'd really been dead I'd have felt it, and I've felt nothing at all. Of course, poor Andie was quite mad when he wrote that letter. As if he could have murdered anybody. Are you hungry? These are excellent sandwiches."

Douglas patted her on the shoulder and she beamed happily at him like a young child who has just been noticed by a beloved adult.

"That's just what I'd like," he said, and helped himself to a sandwich. "Mr. Hunnicut—" He turned to the small man, holding out his hand. "I've been hearing so much about you lately, I think it's time we met."

Walter Hunnicut took a long, thoughtful look at the

hand held out to him, then deliberately tightened the hold that he had with both his own on the back of the chair.

"I think it's time I left," he said. "I don't want to intrude on your hospitality."

"But you didn't mind doing it when you thought I was dead," Douglas said. "We've met somewhere, isn't that correct? Forgive me if I don't remember it, but I've never been any good at faces."

Elspeth had sprung to her feet. She launched herself at Douglas, threw her arms round his neck and covered his face with kisses.

"I thought you were *dead—dead—dead!*" Another kiss followed each repetition of the word.

He made a grimace. "Will no one rid me of this troublesome child?" he demanded, trying to hold her away.

She began to giggle hysterically, kissed him again, then let him go, suddenly began to weep noisily and fled from the room.

"Douglas, that wasn't kind," Frances said. "The poor child's been in agony, believing you were dead. She isn't used to death."

"But the rest of you haven't been in agony, have you?" he said. "Irene now—she looks just a bit put out at my having turned up, as if someone she wasn't expecting had arrived to dinner and she wasn't sure if it would upset her seating arrangements. And Mr. Hunnicut . . . Well, Mr. Hunnicut, here I am. What do you want with me?"

Walter Hunnicut did not hurry to reply. His eyes looked more than usually hard and calculating.

Irene floundered to her feet.

"I don't understand what's been happening," she said, "but I must go and see what that child's doing. I must say, I think you might be kinder to her, Douglas. She hero-worships you. Is that so hard to put up with? And I must say too, if you weren't dead, it wasn't very nice of you to let us go on thinking you were."

"The news of my death was only broken to me half an hour ago or less," he said. "As soon as I heard, I hurried here as fast as I could to let you know you hadn't inherited Havershaw. No one could have been more considerate."

"Saying silly things like that doesn't help at all," Irene said. She yawned. "Oh God, I'm so tired. It's been a dreadful day. Frances dear, I'll go and see if your clothes are dry."

She stalked out of the room.

"She's quite right, of course, Douglas," Frances said. "This isn't the time for bad jokes. Because poor Andie really is dead. And Mr. Hunnicut, who thought you'd murdered his wife, now thinks it was Andie all along, because of some ear-rings the police found in the lodge, which apparently belonged to her. Whatever the truth of everything is, the one thing that's certain is that it's all very, very sad."

Douglas sat down beside her on the sofa and took one of her short, strong hands in his.

"You're right, you always are," he said. "And you're right to tell me off. You're the one person from whom I've never minded it."

"Because you think I'm mad," she said. "A lot of people do, so they don't think there's any need to take me seriously. But I always mean everything I say. Now you'd better telephone the police to tell them you're alive, because it will save the poor men a lot of trouble, hunting for your dead body, which is what they're very busy doing."

"All right." Douglas stood up. "Mr. Hunnicut, if you don't mind waiting a little, we can have a talk later."

Walter Hunnicut did not look as if he wanted to remain. He looked rather as a person does who has dropped in casually to visit friends, to find that a party is in progress to which he has not been invited, and no matter how pressing the invitations are then that he should stay, can think only of how to get away again as quickly as possible.

Catherine and Brian had come into the room. Frances inquired how they had discovered Douglas and Catherine told her how they had found him sitting by the pool, as well as how Douglas had told them how he had spent the day in London, trying to find ways of showing his gratitude to Andie for saving his life.

"He didn't even know that Andie was dead," she said. "He says they had a row last night and Andie got very drunk and passed out and Douglas put him on the couch to sleep it off. And Brian thinks Andie came half round and couldn't really remember what had happened except that there'd been a fight, and thought he'd killed Douglas and so went and killed himself."

"I didn't say I thought that," Brian said. "I only said that's how it could have happened."

"Then what *do* you think happened?" Walter Hunnicut asked.

Brian's rather absentminded gaze dwelt on his face for a moment.

"I think Andie was murdered," he said. "Perhaps by someone who knows more about him than he wants us to think. Unless, of course, Douglas did it. But I don't know why he should, unless he's got tired of Andie living on him, or it happened accidentally during that row they had. But there's not much point in trying to guess until after the post mortem. At the moment we don't even know if Andie died of drowning or what."

Douglas came back into the room.

"Chase wants me to go along to the police station in Newelbury," he said. "Besides showing him that I'm really alive, he wants me to account for my actions all day. I'll have to drive over at once. So we can't do much talking now, Mr. Hunnicut. You do want to talk to me, don't you? I understand that's why you've been hanging around Biddingfold. I'm sorry I've been so unavailable. But I can at least give you a lift to your hotel and perhaps you can say most of what you want to on the way."

Walter Hunnicut did not answer. He was still returning Brian's gaze, as if he were thinking over what he had said, but his face had suddenly become very white. He seemed to be deliberately avoiding looking at Douglas.

Then all of a sudden he turned his head and the two men looked at one another.

Fear, sharper than she had ever known in her life, struck coldly at Catherine. She had never seen before what she was looking at now on the face of Walter Hunnicut, pure, undisguised hatred. She had seen anger, spite, malice on human faces, but the shock of seeing the lust simply to kill transform a face that she knew was something that she had never experienced. In that high, glittering, formal room it was as if an animal out of the jungle had got loose.

Neither man spoke to the other. Neither of them snarled, neither growled. Yet the air seemed to reverberate with the roar with which the big carnivore terrifies its prey. A strangeness about that moment was that there was a certain pale terror on the face of the small man, as if to realise what was convulsing him was more than he could bear.

"Thank you, I'll walk home," he said.

"On the other hand," Douglas said, "you could wait here till I get back. I don't suppose they'll keep me long in Newelbury."

"I'm sure the people here would prefer to be left in peace."

"Suppose I look in at your hotel then—the Green Man, is it?—on my way back."

"I don't think there'd be much to be gained by it. I think I shall have a drink and go to bed."

Words were neutralising the rage in the room. The jungle animals after all could speak. Roaring was unnecessary.

"Of course you should get into some dry clothes," Douglas said. "Our climate isn't like the one you're used to. You could easily get a chill. Are you sure you wouldn't like a lift?"

"Thank you, a walk will warm me up." Walter Hunnicut moved away from the chair on which he had been leaning. As he removed his arms from it, it seemed to surprise him to see a damp patch on the velvet where his sleeves had rested. "But just tell me this, Mr. Cable, how long have you known that Manson killed my wife?"

"Your wife?" Douglas looked puzzled.

"My wife, June. June Hunnicut."

"Oh—*June.*" There was a startled sound in Douglas's voice. "She was your wife? June. I didn't know. I don't think I ever heard her other name. It isn't one I'd have forgotten, is it? I just knew her as June, the few times I met her. And I didn't know that Andie . . . Are you sure? How can you be sure?"

"He had her ear-rings," Walter Hunnicut said. "I think the police will show them to you, if you ask them."

Douglas shook his head. "It sounds a bit flimsy. I don't

know anything about it—whatever really happened. I did meet this girl called June who was a friend of Andie's, but that he murdered her—no, I don't believe it. I'm sorry, very sorry, whatever the truth is, but there's no reason for you to believe I've been covering up a murder all this time. There's no reason"—he smiled for the first time since he had come into the room—"why you shouldn't let me give you a lift to the Green Man."

"I'll give Mr. Hunnicut a lift, if he wants one," Brian said. "I'll be taking Catherine and Frances home anyway. I've room for a fourth."

"Oh goodness, dearie, then I must rush and change," Frances said. "I can't go off in Irene's best dressing-gown. Can you wait a few minutes, Brian, while I change?"

Brian said of course, but Walter Hunnicut repeated that he would prefer to walk. They stood about silently, waiting for Frances to return.

There was a bleakness in the silence which made the apparent peace of the moment seem deeply unreal to Catherine. If it was not as formidable as what had gone before, it had a hollowness that gave the room the feeling of some cold, underground cavern, the brightness of which was false. The darkness outside, behind the yellow curtains, was the reality.

Sensing her mood, Brian put an arm round her shoulders and gave her arm a squeeze, as if he were trying to convey some message to her. A message simply of comfort and reassurance. She felt a light-headed and wonderful clarity about her feeling for him.

Presently Frances came in, wearing the cotton dress that she had worn all day, a mass of creases, but dry.

"It's so good of you to drive me home, Brian," she said. "I'm so tired, I don't think I could struggle along that path. Apart from the feeling that I don't want to walk past that pool. If you'll take my advice, Douglas, you'll get it filled in and plant a rose garden there again. The place is going to be haunted by you as well as by Andie, even though you're alive. It will be, you know. It'll be a bad-luck place. Now let's go."

She led the way out into the passage and along it to the door that opened into the garage.

Outside in the moonlight they could see Brian's car, the Lotus and the Rolls. The garage itself was empty.

Frances went towards Brian's car. Catherine followed her and Brian went beside Catherine. Douglas hesitated. He seemed uncertain whether to drive into Newelbury in the Lotus or the Rolls. Then he started towards the Rolls.

Frances gave a hoarse cry.

She raced to him and flung her arms round him. He hit out at her blindly. Reeling and staggering on the gravel beside the car, making meaningless, snorting noises at one another, the two of them seemed to be fighting.

Then all of a sudden Douglas stood still, laughing and apologising.

"Oh, Frances, I'm so sorry. You took me by surprise. I completely lost my head. But for God's sake, what's all this about?"

"The car, the car!" Frances cried. "Don't you understand, that's how he did it? He wrote that he'd murdered you, didn't he? That he'd done it already. That's because he'd fixed your car. The Rolls. He may have known you'd be going to London. He thought you'd take the Rolls. If I were you, I wouldn't get into that car till the police have been over it. My guess is, if you do, it'll go off like a bomb."

CHAPTER TEN

The police came.

They came unexpectedly quickly after Douglas's telephone call to Mr. Chase and they took Frances's idea about a bomb in the Rolls with a seriousness that surprised Catherine.

She thought that it also surprised Douglas. He had made the telephone call reluctantly and it had only been the strength of the grip on him that Walter Hunnicut and Brian had taken between them that had stopped him thrusting his way into the car to drive it back into the garage. Scoffingly then he had agreed to call the police, who had not scoffed, but had told him not to let anyone go near the car and to get everyone in the house out of it as quickly as possible and to assemble them at some distance from it.

There was bewilderment on his face as he relayed this message to the people still waiting near the car.

"Believe it or not, they want the house evacuated!" he exclaimed. "And all because of a nutty idea of Frances's." He turned to her. "Do you know something about this, or is it just a crazy guess?"

Walter Hunnicut answered for her. "I guess it's just a crazy guess, unless you'd sooner call it logic. Manson said he'd murdered you. Said it was done. Yet you aren't dead. But that doesn't mean he hadn't fixed things so that you'd be dead enough shortly. And I'd say Miss Knox is right, that could mean just two things—two things that could work out quite satisfactorily after he was dead himself—bombs or poison."

Douglas made a whistling sound through his teeth. "I've always thought of logic as a dull sort of thing. Perhaps I'll have to think again. Now I'd better get hold of Irene to get her to get this evacuation organised. Brian, what about you keeping a watch on the car to see no one goes near it? And the rest of you go out on the lawn and I'll see that all the others join you, a bloody load of rubbish though I think it is. I think I could drive that car into the garage and no one be any the worse."

"In that case, try it," Walter Hunnicut suggested. "But give the rest of us time to get clear."

He and Douglas exchanged a long, challenging look.

"Is that what you hope I'll do?" Douglas asked. "Do you want to goad me into doing just that?"

"Do you goad that easily?"

"Douglas, dearie, if you're not going looking for Irene to get the house emptied out," Frances said, "I am. The police didn't laugh at you when you talked about a bomb in the Rolls and they aren't fools. I think we ought to hurry about getting everyone out of the house."

"You're right, of course."

Douglas went indoors, calling out to Irene.

Frances, Walter Hunnicut and Catherine returned through the house to the terrace, while Brian stayed behind to keep a watch on the car. Presently Irene, Elspeth, Mrs. Forsyth and the two other servants, both Portuguese girls, who slept in, came out to join the group on the terrace. Except for Irene, they were all in dressing-gowns and were puzzled and rather querulous and inclined to mutter that they had had enough of the police for one day.

Even Elspeth, who normally had a love of drama, looked sullen at having been roused. Yet she seemed more afraid than any of the others and stayed close to her mother, sitting down beside her on one of the benches and taking her hand.

Douglas had not appeared on the terrace, so Catherine supposed that he had gone to join Brian. Mrs. Forsyth and the two Portuguese girls sat down in a group at a little distance from the others, stiffly careful of social differences. Walter Hunnicut roamed away across the lawn, then began to walk up and down, as if wanting to make a point of the fact that he did not belong to the household, or was even a guest. Frances, settling herself on one of the garden chairs, let her head droop forward on her chest and began to snore gently.

From the terrace they all heard the police come, the sound of voices and of footsteps crunching the gravel of the drive.

Presently Brian emerged from the house.

"At least one mystery's solved," he said. "Why the police took Frances's theory about a bomb in the Rolls so seriously. It seems they found some gelignite in Andie's shed. Douglas didn't know he had it, though he knew where it came from. It was some of the stuff left over from what he got hold of to blast those chestnuts they brought down when he was having the swimming pool built. He said he didn't even know there was any left over and hasn't any idea when Andie took it. Meanwhile, the police aren't touching the car. They're waiting for the bomb disposal people to arrive."

"And what are we supposed to do while they're waiting?" Irene asked petulantly. "Just go on sitting here? I think there's a change coming in the weather. It's much colder than it was. We'll all get chills if we simply sit here."

"Better than getting blown to bits, anyway," Brian said. "I'd try to be patient."

"Why don't you come home with me?" Catherine suggested. "The police can be told where we've gone."

"That's an excellent idea," Brian said. "Go along with Catherine, Irene, and I'll follow with Douglas as soon as the police say we can go."

"Go all that way in our dressing-gowns?" Mrs. Forsyth said in a scandalised voice.

"Oh come, you're much more covered up than most of you are in the daytime," Brian said.

Frances sat up with a start. "Yes, yes, but why don't you all come home to me? I'd love to have you. And there's plenty to drink in the house, gin, whisky, sherry, vodka..."

Brian patted her shoulder. "It was Catherine's idea. You just go along with her."

"I no go past that pool in the dark!" one of the Portuguese girls cried. "I no go for nothing!"

Walter Hunnicut, who had rejoined the group to hear what Brian had to say, took her arm and hauled her to her feet.

"I'll be with you, sweetheart, you needn't be afraid of anything," he said, and reaching for the arm of the other girl, placed himself between them. "There now, no one's afraid, are they?"

He led the way across the lawn towards the pool.

The Cookhams heard the party arrive and emerged from their quarters in the old house to find out what was happening. They had been watching television and had not yet gone to bed. Catherine tried to tell them briefly what had happened. But too much had happened. It was impossible to be brief. She was relieved when Mrs. Cookham gave her an understanding look, linked her arm through one of Mrs. Forsyth's, from whom it was more likely that she would hear more of the gruesome details of what had happened during the last two or three hours than she would from Catherine, and drew her away to her own living room. The two women had become friends during the short time that Mrs. Forsyth had worked for the Cables. They took the two Portuguese girls with them, promising them tea and cake. Catherine led the way to her own living room, brought out drinks, then went to the kitchen and started cutting sandwiches to supplement those made by Mrs. Forsyth earlier in the evening.

Douglas and Brian arrived together about half an hour later. Douglas said Chase would be along as soon as he had anything to report. He was subdued but restless. He sat down, stood up, roamed about, wrenched at his tie as if it were choking him, sat down again and, reaching for Andie's carving of the small, crouching man, nursed it between both hands, studying it thoughtfully.

"The bloody man had talent," he muttered. "Why did he have to go and do what he did? You going to keep this, Catherine?"

"Why not?" she said.

"Even if Hunnicut's right and Andie was a murderer? I'd have thought you might find it an upsetting thing to have around."

"I don't know how I'm going to feel about it when I've got used to what's happened," she answered.

"Well, if you find it getting you down, I'll take it off your hands," Douglas said. "I'm keeping the things I managed to save last night when he went for them with a hammer. And I think this is one of the best things he's done."

"You don't think you'll be got down by them then," Walter Hunnicut said. He was standing near Douglas, looking at the mannikin in his hands.

"Oh, I'm not going to keep them around," Douglas said. "They're going out of sight into a drawer or a trunk. One day they'll be valuable." He looked up at the other man. "Do you still think I killed your wife?"

The small man moved away from him to the window.

"Don't worry about me, anyway," he said. "I'm leaving. I'm going home."

"When the police let you go," Brian reminded him.

"*If* they let me go, isn't that what you mean?" the small man said.

No one answered that. There was silence in the room except for an occasional little snuffling snore from Frances, who had dropped off again into a doze.

Douglas put Andie's carving down again, but went on looking at it as if it hypnotised him.

Presently he said, "How long do you have to know a man before you can be sure you know anything about him?"

"I should think that depends more on you than on him," Brian said.

"I've known Andie a dozen years. He was just a kid when I knew him first. He used to hang around me, getting me to tell him stories of England. I used to make most of them up, because I didn't remember all that much. I thought I knew all there was to know about him."

Frances gave a slightly louder honk than usual and sat up with a jerk.

"I believe I've been asleep," she said.

Catherine patted her hand. "I'd go back to sleep, if I were you."

"But I heard what you were saying—something about how much you don't know about people you think you've known for years. Yes, it all depends on you, of course. Some people are so blind. I'm very intuitive myself. You'd be surprised how much I know. But knowledge is a burden. Such a responsibility."

Her eyelids drooped again and after a moment she gave another little snore.

Irene gave a sharp sigh. "This waiting is horrible. I feel awful. I don't believe there's anything the matter with that car. I'm dreadfully tired. I want to go to bed. I don't believe the police have any right to stop me."

"Only I'm sure you'd sooner be here if Havershaw is going up with a bang," Douglas said.

"It isn't, it isn't!" Elspeth cried hysterically. "Not Havershaw. I couldn't bear that. I'd die. Anyway, how could Andie possibly have made a bomb if he was as drunk as you say?"

"How indeed?" Brian said. "A very shrewd point."

"Well, here are the police now," Catherine said, going to the front door, outside of which she had heard voices and footsteps. "They'll tell us the worst."

She opened the door.

Mr. Chase advanced into the room.

"If Mr. Cable had opened that car door," he said, "he'd have been blown sky-high. And I think most of the garage would have gone up with him and a good hole blown in the side of the house."

Douglas did not look up. He went on staring at the little wooden figure, so calmly benign, on the coffee table. It was as if he felt that only from it was any understanding to be had of what had been happening.

"Frances, I haven't said it yet—thank you," he said.

She went on snoring quietly.

"I hope she'll have better luck than the last one who saved your life," Walter Hunnicut said. "Someone seems to want you dead and doesn't take it kindly when his plans are interfered with."

"Then you don't believe it was Andie who set that bomb," Douglas said. "Why not?"

"Because I think Miss Wilde's right," Walter Hunnicut answered. "If he was as drunk as we've been told, he wouldn't have been capable of constructing a bomb and getting it fixed in your car this morning."

"There are other reasons for doubting it," Mr. Chase said.

Douglas looked up at him with a startled air, as if he had only just become aware of his presence in the room.

"I'll be glad to hear them," he said. "Andie was an old friend. I'd sooner be able to go on thinking of him as the man who saved my life on Friday than as the one who tried to kill me today."

"Well, I'd be grateful if you'd tell me about your movements this morning," Mr. Chase said. "What time did you leave for London?"

"About seven-thirty," Douglas answered.

"Did anyone see you?"

"I don't think so."

"Didn't anyone bring you breakfast?"

"One of the girls brought tea to my room and after that I didn't bother with breakfast. I had a snack later on the way to London."

"And you went in the Lotus?"

"Yes."

"Why not in the Rolls?"

"The Lotus is more manoeuvreable in traffic. It's easier to park."

"Yet you drove the Rolls out of the garage and left it in the drive. Why did you do that?"

"It was automatic. I began by thinking I'd go in the Rolls and drove it into the drive. Then I remembered I really prefer the Lotus when I go to London, so I changed over from one car to the other and didn't bother to put the Rolls back in the garage, but just drove off."

"Leaving the car unlocked and the key in the ignition."

"I believe I did. Careless of me, but it always seems so safe here."

"And this was at about seven-thirty?"

"I didn't look at my watch, that I remember, but I should think it was about then."

"So the Rolls was perfectly safe for you to drive at that time."

"Yes, certainly."

"So whoever put the bomb in it did it some time after seven-thirty."

Douglas was frowning. "Yes, that must be right," he said.

"However, Dr. Farquahar thinks Mr. Manson had been dead at least eighteen hours when his body was discovered. Not that he can say much definitely yet, but that's his impression. Incidentally, you were right, Mrs. Cable, the reason the gardeners didn't find him is that they were at work in the vegetable garden all day. And he died by drowning, though he may have been unconscious when he went into the pool. There are bruise marks all over him, particularly on his face and chest."

Douglas drew a hand across his face, the gesture of someone trying to brush away a painful thought.

"I may be responsible for those," he said. "I told you, we had a fight last night. We met here in Miss Gifford's house and I wanted to thank him for having saved me. I hadn't seen him since it happened. But somehow he turned quarrelsome. I think perhaps he'd been drinking already. And when we got to the lodge together he went on, and then started abusing me because he thought I was trying to take Miss Gifford away from him. He was quite wrong, as it happens, but it may have been my fault that he thought so."

"What happened then?"

"Oh, he went on drinking and then got violent. Only he didn't attack me, he started smashing up his own work, shouting out that it was no good and that I'd never believed in him and no one else was going to either. So I tried to stop him. I did believe in him. I admire his work immensely. So I had to knock him out to stop him destroying it all."

"I thought you said before he passed out from the drink he'd had," Brian said.

"Well, it was really a bit of each. He wouldn't have gone down so easily from the knock I gave him if it hadn't been for the drink. And when I saw I'd laid him out I put him on the couch, collected as many of his sculptures as I could carry and took them to Havershaw, to keep them out of harm's way. And this morning I took some of them up to London with me to see if I could persuade a man I know to give him a show, and I think I succeeded, only now—now, of course—" His voice went hoarse again and dried up.

"Now tell me just one thing more, Mr. Cable," Mr. Chase said. "Have you still no memory of who hit you on the head on Friday and left you to drown in the pool?"

Douglas did not answer at once, then shook his head gravely.

"It's a dead blank, you know. I'm sorry."

"Nothing at all has come back to you?"

"Nothing. Perhaps actually there's nothing to come. I mean, if whoever it was, if it was anybody, crept up behind me and I never saw him, I could hardly remember him, could I?"

"No. Well, I'll leave you in peace now. You must all be very tired. The Rolls has been removed, as evidence, and the house is quite safe now—unless any other booby traps have been set."

Douglas got to his feet. He gave a weary smile.

"That's a cheerful thought to end on. I hope it doesn't keep anyone awake."

"The bomb, by the way, was a fairly crude kind," the superintendent said, "but it would probably have taken several hours to make. So either someone worked hard last night, after disposing of Mr. Manson and setting him up as a scapegoat with that letter and planting the remains of the gelignite in his shed, or else he got the bomb and the letter ready beforehand and was waiting for a favourable opportunity for using them. In any case, Mr. Cable, I'd take a certain amount of care for the present about such things as swimming alone and leaving the keys in your car. And if anything—anything at all—about that attack on Friday comes back to you, get in touch with me at once. I think what happened on Friday is the main clue to the murder of your friend Manson, and it's very important for us to find out what happened then."

Douglas put a hand to the back of his head, grimacing as if a spot there were still sore.

"All right, if I remember anything, I'll tell you," he promised.

"Good night then," Mr. Chase said, and he and the other policemen who had waited outside drove away.

After a little aimless talk, the others all left too, Elspeth collecting Mrs. Forsyth and the two girls from the Cookhams' half of the house, and Walter Hunnicut seeing the drowsy Frances home. Only Brian stayed, going with the others as far as the gate, then turning back into the house and helping himself to some whisky and a sandwich.

"Want me to go too," he asked, "or can I stay for a little?"

"Oh, stay," she said. "Please stay."

He put down the whisky and the sandwich and took her in his arms. He explored her face gently with his mouth, lingering on her eyelids, only just touching her lips.

"You're very tired," he said.

"Not too tired."

"I won't stay long—not tonight. But there's a question I want to ask you—"

"No more questions!" she cried. "It's been nothing but questions ever since Friday."

"Just one," he said. "Do we get married?"

"Oh, yes, please."

"I'm afraid after all that leads to another question. When?"

"As soon as we can, of course."

"You mean we just slip away into Newelbury in a day or two with a couple of witnesses and sign a document and that's it?"

"Yes."

"You don't want a wedding-dress, bridesmaids, the works? Be honest now. Say what you want."

"No, I think I'd like Frances for a witness, it'd make her so happy. And—let me see—Irene, perhaps. Whom do you want?"

"Anyone you choose. I'll go into Newelbury tomorrow and get the licence. But you're sure that's how you want it? Women are supposed to want veils and bouquets and receptions and everything."

"Even when they've got a murder on their hands?"

"There's that, of course."

He let her go, returned to his whisky and sandwich and sat down, looking at her.

"Catherine, my darling, can you bear it if I ask you still another question?" he asked.

She smiled. "It's all right," she said, "I knew you would."

"Douglas talks as if he and Andie quarrelled because Andie thought he was coming between the two of you. Is there any truth in it?"

"Is that jealousy talking, or the detective mind?"

"About half and half, I'd say."

She sat down on the sofa, kicked her shoes off and put her feet up.

"D'you know, that's been on my mind all day," she said. "And the trouble is, I don't know the answer. Until that quarrel started here it never occurred to me that Douglas had the slightest interest in me. And this evening—well, did he act as if he had? We've been good enough friends, but I've always thought it stopped there. But yesterday evening he seemed to go out of his way to make Andie think that he and I had some sort of affair going. Instead of trying to calm Andie down when he seemed to be showing signs of jealousy, he struck me as trying to get under Andie's skin to make things worse. And each of them seemed to be threatening the other in some way. It was very strange. About Andie, Brian . . ."

"There's no need to talk of him," Brian said. "Poor devil."

"But I want to. I really was in love with him for a time, you know."

"Anyone could see that."

"I found him awfully exciting. Different from anyone I knew. But I always held back, I didn't really understand the reason. Well, of course, you were the reason, I know that now, and I'm glad I found it out in time, before I blundered into something really stupid."

"Like having an affair with him?"

"Perhaps. I just don't know what I might have done. I think I might have thrown up my job and gone away and perhaps never seen you again."

Brian crossed the room to her and stretched out on the sofa beside her, resting his head between her breasts.

"Has it occurred to you," he said, "that whoever fixed the bomb in the Rolls must have realised the Lotus was gone and that Douglas was probably in it?"

"Brian!"

"What's wrong now?"

"Are we making love or just playing detectives?"

"Which do you want?"

"Do you have to ask?"

He left about an hour later. It was only after he had gone that Catherine realised that Mrs. Cookham must have been listening for the sound of his departure, for the front door had hardly closed behind him when there came a knock at the door of Catherine's living room and Mrs. Cookham, in a baby-pink cotton housecoat, with rollers in her hair, came into the room.

"Am I disturbing you, dear?" she said. "It won't take a minute, but there's something I've got to say to you. I don't think I'll sleep if I don't."

Catherine was in a dream. She felt glowing with vitality, yet half asleep. She gave an expansive yawn, which sent ripples of pleasure through her.

"What is it, Mrs. Cookham?"

"It's what Mrs. Forsyth's been saying to me," Mrs. Cookham said. "I don't know if I've done right, giving her the advice I did."

"I'm sure you have," Catherine said, feeling that Mrs. Cookham was one of the people who inevitably do right on almost every occasion, that it may be a very limited right, not lit by imagination, not framed to cope with subtleties, but nevertheless basically sound, basically good.

"It's about Miss Wilde," Mrs. Cookham said.

"Oh." That startled Catherine. She rubbed her eyes and tried to concentrate. "What about her?"

"It's just that Mrs. Forsyth saw her, you see, on Friday, coming up from the pool to the house."

"But of course she did. She and Mrs. Cable went up together."

"No, it wasn't like that. Mrs. Forsyth saw them coming up from the pool together and go off to their rooms to change, and then a little while later, when Mrs. Forsyth happened to look out of the window again, there was Miss Wilde again, coming up from the pool and running as fast as she could. Mrs. Forsyth didn't think anything about it at the time. She thought Miss Wilde had forgotten a towel or something and was in a hurry because guests were coming. And even when she heard how someone had hit Mr. Cable on the head and knocked him into the pool, she didn't think much about what she'd seen, because she didn't think a girl like Miss Wilde could have done a thing like that, and anyway, Mrs. Forsyth naturally didn't want to get mixed up with the police herself. So she didn't say anything about it. But now, with Mr. Manson dying in the pool and all this story of a bomb in Mr. Cable's Rolls Royce, she's begun to wonder if she hasn't done wrong to say nothing. So we talked it over and I've advised her to speak to Mrs. Cable about it in the morning, and I promised her I'd speak to you."

Catherine was fully awake again. The dream of the last hour faded.

"You don't mean you think Miss Wilde knocked Mr. Cable on the head, and when that didn't work, planted a bomb in his car!" she exclaimed.

"No . . . No, that isn't what I meant exactly," Mrs. Cookham said uncertainly. "I can't see Miss Wilde knowing how to make a bomb. But . . ." She fiddled with one of the rollers in her hair. "She *could* have hit him on the head, couldn't she? The police said a woman could have done that. And Mr. Redmayne—well, he's a very practical gentleman, isn't he? He knows all about guns and explosives and that. He must, living the life he does. And if he marries Miss Wilde and Mrs. Cable inherits Havershaw from Mr. Cable, well, Mrs. Cable always gives Miss Wilde everything she wants, so you can't say Mr. Redmayne hasn't got a motive. So . . ."

She stopped there, leaving Catherine to finish her sentence.

Catherine did not finish it. She had had just such thoughts of Nick herself. They were no surprise to her, though she had not thought of Elspeth as an accomplice. Among the people she knew, it seemed to her that Nick was much the best suspect. Almost too good a suspect, in fact. For if he were a murderer, surely he would have covered his tracks more cleverly than he had. He was not a stupid man.

She gave a thoughtful nod but said nothing and after a moment Mrs. Cookham went away.

CHAPTER ELEVEN

That night Catherine fell quickly into an uneasy half sleep. Things that had happened and things that she had heard pounded on her brain with an insistence that frightened her, making her feel that it was now, in the quiet darkness of her room, that they were happening.

That quarrel between Andie and Douglas, for instance.

The words that they had said so softly to one another came back to her with what she felt certain was complete accuracy. Yet could you really remember anything so clearly?

She thought that she remembered Douglas saying, "That's something for Catherine herself to decide, isn't it?"

And Andie had answered, "I could make her decide pretty quickly if I wanted to, couldn't I?"

"But what would you gain by doing that? Not her gratitude. I don't think you'd get much of that."

"My own satisfaction then, a bloody lot of satisfaction."

"Which you might find came rather expensive."

"But don't you sometimes want something expensive, Doug, something that's way, way beyond anything you can afford?"

"I'm glad you realise you can't afford it."

"But just remember it could come far too dear for you too, Doug—even for you. A lifetime too dear."

Was that how it had gone? And what had it meant? A

lifetime too dear. . . . A life sentence? For what? The murder of a woman called June?

Next morning the spell of fine weather showed signs of breaking. Some heavy clouds were shouldering their way up the sky. There was a gusty wind blowing that sent sharp little draughts through the old house.

On her way to the surgery one passer-by greeted Catherine with the statement that they'd had their summer and shouldn't expect any more. Another said that it was nice and fresh after that broiling heat and another that you never knew where you were and how were you to know what to put on?

She agreed with them all and hurried on. She was a little late through having sat mooning over her breakfast, trying to decide what she ought to do about Mrs. Cookham's information. But everything that she tried to think about kept melting into memories of Brian and the wonder of still being able to feel so much peace and so much excitement at the same time. She felt guilty about feeling so happy at such a time, the nightmares of the night forgotten, but the feeling was too precious to let go of even for a moment. She nursed it secretly, hoping that she looked normal and not as if she were in the amazing state that she was in.

Yet what Mrs. Cookham had said demanded some decision, some action. Mrs. Cookham, it was plain, had done all that she felt was demanded of her. It was for Catherine, not for Mrs. Cookham, to become involved with the police, if that was necessary for either of them. And Catherine could not decide whether it was or not, for she was not sure if she believed in what Mrs. Forsyth had said she had seen. And even if she really had seen Elspeth running up from the pool a second time, why should it not have been simply because she had forgotten a towel?

Was it possible to believe that Elspeth had made a murderous attack on Douglas on Friday, and that, having failed then, she had tried again, with the help of Nicholas Redmayne, to kill not only Douglas, but Andie as well? Was that the kind of thing about which you rang up Mr. Chase and said that you simply had to see him?

The surgery that morning seemed never ending. The telephone kept on ringing with demands for appointments, for renewals of prescriptions, for confidential chats with Catherine about matters which the patients felt were not important enough to trouble the doctor about. The time passed slowly with what seemed to be one triviality after another.

Not that any of the troubles described would seem trivialities to the people concerned. But there was not enough drama in anything that happened to take Catherine's mind off the problem posed to her by Mrs. Cookham, though there was enough distraction to stop her thinking constructively about it. When Catherine finally left the surgery and went to the butcher to buy a chop for her evening meal, she had more or less decided to say nothing to the police about Mrs. Cookham's revelation. For what Mrs. Forsyth had said to Mrs. Cookham and Mrs. Cookham said to Catherine was hardly evidence.

Loyalty to Irene had something to do with this decision. The two of them should at least talk it over, Catherine thought, before she did anything. She went into the butcher's, and there came face to face with Nick, who was just buying some kidneys.

It was seldom easy to guess from Nick's heavy, expressionless face what he thought, but Catherine had the feeling that if the shop had been larger he would have contrived not to see her, hurrying out before she had a chance to speak to him. As it was, he only muttered,

"Hallo—lousy day—this bloody climate—" and plunged past her through the door.

Yet when she came out of the shop a few minutes later, he was in the street, waiting for her.

"It's just occurred to me," he said, "if you've the time to spare, I'd like to give you a bit more manuscript. And that's the lot, the end of the thing."

"The book's finished?" she asked.

"Except for this last bit of typing and some revision. Will you be able to get on with it, or have recent events been too distracting? I expect I can find someone to do the job for me in London if you don't think you can cope. But the fact is, I'm in a hurry. I'm starting a lecture tour next week—I'm going to America—and I've a good deal of preparation to do."

"I'd like to get on with it," Catherine said. "I need something to do."

"Good. Then come along now and pick up the stuff."

They walked together towards his cottage.

It felt very strange to be walking along beside someone whom she half suspected of murder. She ought, she thought, to have felt at least a little afraid. But instead, she found her suspicions becoming even less convincing than they had been before, almost nebulous, and her relationship with Nick seemed to be exactly what it had always been.

"You've never spoken of this lecture tour before," she said.

"No, well, I wasn't sure if I wanted to take it on. I wasn't sure if I wanted to go away just at the moment. Now I know I do and you know why. It's this trouble with Elspeth. Far the best thing for me to do is to go away."

"Oh, but . . ." She stopped, not knowing what she had been about to say.

"Oh, *but!*" he echoed her savagely. "Don't *you* say I'm being a fool. Don't say I'm to blame if we bust things up. You saw yourself what happened yesterday."

He opened the cottage door and Catherine went ahead of him into the tiny sitting room.

With the clouds slowly piling up to cover the sky and a sense of moisture in the air, as if rain were coming soon, there was no temptation to go out to the little courtyard at the back. Nick swept a pile of notes off a chair to make room for Catherine to sit down.

"She's never cared for me, you know," he said. "I think everyone knows it. She only tried to make use of me when she couldn't make any headway with Douglas. And because it didn't work she's begun to blame me for it, as if it might have worked, you know, if I'd been someone more impressive." He was speaking faster as the bitterness in his voice increased. "But I don't take to being used and I don't like being made to look ridiculous."

"What I'm puzzled about," Catherine said, "since you put it like that, is what she's ever meant to you."

"What's puzzling about it? I was in love with her."

"Were you?"

"Sufficiently."

"That's a dreadfully inadequate answer."

He sat down at the table, facing her.

"All right, perhaps not so very much then. Perhaps not at all. Perhaps nothing you'd recognise as love. It may have been just a change for me that someone seemed to need me, which is odd when I've spent so much of my life taking care that nobody should. Having no one dependent on me, being dependent on no one, that's seemed to me the formula for making life tolerable. Yet when it happened with that beautiful child, of all people, I found I liked it. And if she'd really needed me for anything but her silly little wish to get at Douglas, I don't think you'd have started wondering about my feeling for her. I think it would have become all that it should have been."

"Has she told you that she's in love with Douglas?"

He gave a grim little laugh. "Of course not."

"Then how can you be so sure she is?"

"I'm not sure of it at all. As a matter of fact, I'm sure she isn't."

She wrinkled her forehead. "I don't understand. I thought you said . . ."

"My dear girl, there's only one thing Elspeth loves," he said, "and that's Havershaw. Have you never realised that?"

She leant back in her chair, still frowning as she studied his face. It was more animated than usual. It looked more as if it were made of normal materials, of skin and muscle, with bone behind them, than it usually did. She wondered if it took anger to bring it to life, if pain, humiliation and jealousy were strong stimulants to him.

"I've realised she loved Havershaw," she said, "but not to the exclusion of everything else."

"Oh yes, it's a very exclusive passion," he said. "Just think it out. She came there as an infant, didn't she, when her stepfather died and old Mrs. Cable offered Irene and her child a home? And Elspeth grew up as if she were a daughter of the house, although she always knew she wasn't. She'd nothing to worry about where money was concerned. Mrs. Cable divided what she had between the sons of her husband's two brothers and Irene of course inherited Owen's share. And everything that Irene possesses is Elspeth's. That much you must have noticed, surely. But the house was left to the elder nephew, Douglas, who'd been taken away to Australia by his parents. A complete stranger, descending on Elspeth and Irene and taking charge and changing everything. But being very generous too, realising the two of them had always felt Havershaw was their home and telling them they were welcome to stay on there. Do you disagree with anything I've said so far?"

Catherine shook her head.

"After all," Nick went on, "you must have noticed that whatever Elspeth tried in the way of a job, she always gave up the training after a few months and came home again. At first, when I got to know her, I used to think it was a rather serious case of a mother fixation. But gradually it dawned on me it was the house that held her. She wanted to live in it and be the lady of it. Of course, it's a beautiful place and the mere fact that she's always known it would never belong to her may have made her more desperately possessive about it than she would have been if she'd known it was coming to her some day. But one way of getting possession of it, of course, would have been to marry Douglas. There's a sort of incestuous sound about that, but actually they're no relation. And she tried it. Oh, she tried very hard."

"Nick, wait a moment," Catherine said. "You say she used you. I thought you meant to help her score off Douglas because he'd treated her as a child who shouldn't be thinking of marriage. But do you really mean something quite different?"

"Quite different."

"You'll have to explain a bit more."

"Don't you understand, she didn't want anyone thinking she cared too much about Havershaw? Because she'd made certain plans. So she got herself engaged to a man who was going to take her to the other end of the earth. Because that's what we'd decided, you know. We were going away together on those trips of mine. And that's why I thought she needed me, why I was just the person who could really help her. I could take her away and give her something quite new and exciting to take the place of what she'd lost. And then . . . then . . ." He gave a choking kind of laugh. "Then, well, you know what happened."

Catherine remembered her talk with Mrs. Cookham.

"So you seriously believe Elspeth knocked Douglas on the head and left him to drown so that Irene could inherit Havershaw."

"I think it's possible. I know the girl rather well, you see, and as I've told you, she's a completely wild thing."

"And that's why you're in a hurry to get away. It isn't jealousy of her feeling for Douglas, it's just that you've found out you don't much like the idea of marrying a would-be murderess."

"Of course."

"But you can't believe Elspeth managed to drown Andie and fix that bomb in the car."

"Well, no, that's unlikely. She hasn't got the strength for the one or the know-how for the other."

Catherine put her elbows on the table and leant her head on her hands. Her hair fell forward in two wings on either side of her face, closing off her vision of most of the little room. But she could see Nick's fists resting on the table, brown and powerful and both of them marked with odd scars which somehow suggested that they were not unused to violence.

"Suppose someone drowned Andie for her and helped her with the bomb," she said, "someone who's got the know-how."

"That's possible," he said.

"Then let me tell you, it's been suggested to me that you're that person. And it isn't impossible, is it? Because if

I decided not to believe a word you've said to me this morning about your feelings for Elspeth or hers for you, and just thought about the fact that if Douglas died Irene would inherit Havershaw as well as Douglas's share of Mrs. Cable's fortune, I'd realise, of course, that you wouldn't do badly out of marrying Elspeth. And all this talk about how badly she's treated you and how much you want to get away from her could be a smoke-screen that the two of you had decided to put up."

There was a silence. Catherine noticed the heavy hands on the table tighten slightly, then, after a moment, pick up a ball-point pen, wrench at it and snap it in two. It broke with a sound like a shot. The silence went on.

At last Nick said in an unexpectedly friendly tone, "If you really believed that, you'd be a very brave woman, sitting here with me all alone. I'd have enough blood on my hands already to make a little more or less not very important. But you aren't in the least afraid. So I don't think you do believe it."

She gave a sigh and smiled at him. "I wish I knew what I do believe."

"Well, to change the subject," he said, "how do you feel about typing my last chapter for me? Do you feel too suspicious of me to feel happy about doing it?"

He was laughing at her now, or trying to. There was an unsteadiness in his voice that might have come either from suppressed amusement or from nervous tension.

"No, give it to me," she answered. "I'll do it as fast as I can."

"Thank you."

She left the cottage with the manuscript in her shopping bag.

She had not by any means crossed Nick off her list of possible murderers, although that list, such as it was, had next to no reality for her. No one she knew seemed to belong convincingly on it. She was inclined to believe that whoever wanted Douglas dead must have come here out of his past and was someone she had never seen or heard of. Even Walter Hunnicut, who had come out of Douglas's past with his story of a murdered wife, had already become too much of an ordinary human being to her to seem capable of such a fantastic act as murder.

Anyway, wasn't it always the unlikeliest person who was the guilty one?

Who was the unlikeliest person she could think of?

Frances, perhaps.

The thought probably occurred to Catherine only because she happened to be passing Frances's bungalow at the time and she realised, from the sounds coming from it, that Frances was in the grip of one of her cleaning frenzies. Blinds had been drawn up, windows and doors thrown open, the vacuum cleaner roared and above the noise of it Frances could be heard, loudly singing, "'All we like sheep—all we like sheep—have gone a-stray-ay-ay-ay-ay . . .'"

It was not surprising. Frances was always liable to start cleaning her house when her mind was disturbed and certainly enough had happened to disturb it deeply during the last few days.

A trick of the wind brought the sound of her singing unusually clearly into Catherine's living room. In itself it was not unpleasant, but unfortunately Frances's two dogs liked to accompany her when she sang. They would follow her around the house in the wake of the vacuum cleaner, lifting their heads and howling so mournfully that it sounded as if they must be in a state of the deepest spiritual agony. Yet presumably they were enjoying themselves, for if the music caused them so much pain, all they had to do was walk off into the garden.

Catherine, who began to work on Nick's manuscript as soon as she got in, found the curious symphony very distracting. Even though she could drown it partially by the rattle of the keys of her typewriter, the noise from next door kept intruding on her concentration, making her make more mistakes than usual. Then Irene arrived.

Her tall figure was stooping, her hair straggled limply about her face, her long strides, as she came through the door, looked more disjointed than ever. Her eyes had the slightly sunken, staring look of someone who has not slept.

"You're working," she said, seeing Catherine's typewriter and the papers around it. "But I've got to talk to you, Catherine. Do you mind?"

There was a wildness in the way that she looked round the familiar room as if it has somehow totally altered since she had been in it last.

"And if you could manage a drink, I'd be grateful," she said. "I feel so shaky, it's awful. I've had a terrible shock."

"Come and sit down," Catherine said. "Whisky? No water?"

"Thanks, yes." Irene reached for the glass of neat whisky that Catherine handed to her and gulped at it avidly. "D'you know, really I hate whisky, but it's what I need now. Catherine, you know about Elspeth, don't you? About what Mrs. Forsyth saw."

"I know what Mrs. Cookham's told me about it," Catherine answered.

"Yes, well . . ." Irene was trembling, Catherine saw, though the whisky had quickly brought spots of bright colour to her cheeks. "I'm sorry if I'm muddled. I haven't slept. That woman got hold of me last night after we'd all got home and told me she'd seen Elspeth—I'm talking about Friday, you know—she'd seen the two of us come up from the pool together to change, and then when she happened to look out of the window again a little later, she saw Elspeth coming up from the pool again, looking, she said—oh, it doesn't matter how she was looking, but Catherine, what *am* I to do? Elspeth's admitted it to me, you see. I lay awake all night, trying to think what I ought to do, and after breakfast I said I'd got to talk to her and I told her what Mrs. Forsyth said she'd seen, and Elspeth *admitted* it all—said she'd taken an old branch she'd found under the trees and hit Douglas as hard as she could just as he was going to dive. And she said she hated him and she wished she'd killed him, because he'd taken Havershaw from us. And then she began to cry and said she didn't mean any of it and that if Andie hadn't come on the scene immediately and pulled Douglas out, she'd have done it herself. She said she was there among the trees, behind some bushes, when you and Andie came, and she wasn't even sure you hadn't seen her. And she clung to me and said I wouldn't tell anyone, would I? And I promised I wouldn't, but somehow I *can't* just keep it to myself. I've tried all this morning, but I've felt I was going mad. My Elspeth! Is *she* mad, do you think, Catherine? They always say the people closest to them are the last people to notice anything wrong. With mad people, I mean. Do you think she's having a breakdown or something?"

The torrent of words stopped. Irene's glass was empty. Catherine did not know whether it would be best to give her a re-fill or not. Would it calm her or make her disintegrate completely? But Irene held the glass out for more, so Catherine filled it again.

"That awful noise!" Irene said abruptly, giving a

shudder as a gust of wind brought a few bars of Frances's singing more loudly into the room. She was still on the *Messiah*. "'All we like sheep . . .'"

"How d'you stand it?" Irene asked.

"It doesn't happen often," Catherine said. "Frances is probably trying hard to sort something out in her mind. As we all are. I haven't got very far. All I've managed to work out is that if it was Elspeth who hit Douglas on the head on Friday, then he's got another enemy in the neighbourhood, because she couldn't have killed Andie or put the bomb in the Rolls."

Irene's face suddenly crumpled, her eyes flooded and tears poured down her cheeks.

"I know, I know! So she isn't a murderess, is she?" she gasped. "She really isn't. If you and Andie hadn't come along she really would have gone straight in to save Douglas." She put her glass down so clumsily that some of the whisky spilled out of it, grabbed a handkerchief from her sleeve, then did not use it, but sat there with shaking shoulders and let the tears stream. "I've been saying over and over to myself, she couldn't have made the bomb. I couldn't make up my mind about Andie. I thought, she could have tempted him down to the pool for a swim and then done what she did to Douglas—oh, God, I actually thought that about my own child! But she couldn't make a bomb, could she? You don't know how happy I've been about that bomb. I mean, that there's something I can be absolutely certain of."

She drew a deep breath and began to mop at her tears.

"I'm so glad I came," she went on. "You're always so calm. I knew it would do me good to talk to you. But tell me something, do you think there's any need for me to talk to the police about any of this? I did promise Elspeth, after all, and I've broken my promise already, talking to you. But it wouldn't be right to say anything to the police, would it? Of course, it would be different if there were any connection between Elspeth and the bomb, but we've just decided there isn't. And I've been thinking I know what I ought to do. I ought to take her away from here. Right away. Perhaps abroad for a time. Paris. Vienna. Interesting places. She won't want to come, she's so attached to Havershaw, but I'm going to insist it's what would be best for her. I ought to have seen it sooner. There's something unhealthy about her attitude to Douglas, half loving him and half resenting him so terribly, and all the time wishing we had Havershaw to ourselves. I did hope her engagement to Nick might help. I thought if they'd go right away she'd forget all about the place, but I don't think she ever cared about him much. And I've been thinking I might get her to see a psychiatrist. Don't you think that might be a good idea? Some clever man in Vienna or somewhere. Don't you think it would do far more good than letting a young girl like her get into the hands of the police?"

"All right," Catherine said, "I won't say anything to the police either. But get her away, Irene, I really should."

"Yes, yes, I've quite decided that." Irene was capable of sounding very decided when Elspeth was not there to change her mind for her. "And thank you so much for listening and being so sensible. I'll miss you very much when we move away." She reached for her whisky to finish it, then gave a little giggle. "Of course, it's unheard-of luck that Douglas shouldn't remember a thing about being knocked into the pool, because I don't think he'd be very nice about it, you know. I think he might be quite vindictive. He's very generous and good-natured up to a point, but it's only as long as he has his own way."

Catherine thought that she might feel rather vindictive

herself if someone knocked her into a pool, even if they repented of it the next minute.

"The person I'm sorry for is Nick," she said. "I think he's been hurt quite badly."

"Well, yes, of course, it's too bad," Irene said without much interest. "But I'll go home now and tell Elspeth she's got nothing to worry about. And that I'm taking her away. Oh, I do feel so much better now. Thank you."

She dived on Catherine to give her a quick kiss, then shot out of the room.

To the accompaniment of Handel, howling dogs and the undercurrent of Frances's vacuum cleaner, Catherine returned to her typewriter.

She had some bread and cheese and coffee presently, then went on typing. If Nick wanted his work done quickly, he should have it. Handel after a time gave place to Mozart, and Mozart to Schubert lieder. Then at last there was silence, except that it had begun to rain, a soft pitter-patter on the windows. A gauzy grey curtain of rain drifted past them, darkening the earth in the garden that had dried to pale dust during the heat of the last few days, and dimming the evening light. It was almost soothing. Catherine put the cover on her typewriter, went to the telephone and asked for Brian.

His housekeeper told her that he was out.

Catherine found herself wandering restlessly about the house. Now that she had stopped work, now that she was alone, now that the house was no longer invaded by raucous noises from outside, she could think of nothing but Brian and of how this was probably going to go on for the rest of her life. The thought of him would be there, either in the forefront or at the back of her mind, through all the years to come. Or if that were somehow to be interrupted, her heart would probably break. It was a feeling that scared her, while giving her a deeper happiness than she had ever experienced. After ten minutes she thought of telephoning again. But before she could decide to do so, the doorbell rang once more and this time it was Brian himself, who had already started out on his way to her when she had first telephoned.

They went quickly into one another's arms, but almost at once, with his hands still on her shoulders, he thrust her away from him.

"We've got to hurry," he said. "If I'm right, Elspeth's in great danger. If I'm right, that is. I may be stark mad. But in case I'm not, we've got to think what to do."

With his arm round her shoulders, they went into the living room. Catherine switched on a light. It changed the colour of the rainwashed twilight outside to green-streaked indigo.

"So you know about Elspeth," she said. "How did you find out?"

"Do you mean you know too?" he asked. "Did she actually tell you?"

"She told Irene and Irene told me. And Irene made me promise not to tell anyone, and here I am breaking my promise already, just as she did hers."

"So to that extent I'm not mad," he said. "No one told me anything, you see. I worked it out for myself. Just how much did Irene tell you?"

"That it was Elspeth who knocked Douglas into the pool."

"Why?"

"Because she wanted Havershaw."

"Yes, that must have been the reason."

"But she told Irene she'd have rescued him herself if Andie and I hadn't turned up. And Irene says she's going to take her away and send her to a psychiatrist and hopes that's going to sort her out."

"If she'd take her away at once . . . !" He had flung himself down in a chair. "Catherine, I haven't promised anyone I won't tell what I think, and if Irene doesn't get Elspeth away quickly I shall tell the police what I've guessed and hope I can get them to take steps of some sort." He paused, listening. "That's Frances playing, I suppose."

Although Catherine had closed the window against the rain, the sound of Frances playing and singing again came to them faintly.

"'Oh come, all ye faithful,
Joyful and triumphant . . .'"

The usual howling of the dogs accompanied it.

"Wrong time of year to be playing that, isn't it?" Brian said. "Isn't it a Christmas carol?"

"Well, I've had the *Messiah* and the *Marriage of Figaro* and German lieder all day," Catherine said. "Perhaps she's running out of tunes. What do you mean, Brian? Why is Elspeth in danger?"

"Work it out backwards," he said.

Just then the faint music, coming from the bungalow, changed. Frances seemed to be in a less classical frame of mind than usual. She had started playing, "'Boys and girls, come out to play, The moon doth shine as bright as day. . . .'"

"Who was that bomb meant to kill?" Brian went on. "Start from there. We ought to have seen it at once."

The music changed again. There was something hectic and violent in the way that Frances was pounding the chords.

"'Come, come, come and make eyes at me,
Down at the Old Bull and Bush . . .'"

Brian leapt to his feet.

"We're fools," he cried. "Don't you see what she's saying? 'Come!' *'Come*, all ye faithful . . .' *'Come* out to play . . .' *'Come* and make eyes at me . . .' It means Frances is in danger too!"

CHAPTER TWELVE

The rain blew into their faces as they plunged out into the dark.

As they ran they heard Frances still pounding the piano. Then they heard what sounded like two shots. They were followed immediately by a wild crash of discords as if something heavy had fallen on to the keyboard. Then the music stopped.

The dogs were silent too. Usually they would have started barking at the sound of running feet approaching the bungalow, but no sound came from it.

Brian pressed the bell at the door. It pealed shrilly inside the house but no one came to answer it and the dogs still did not bark.

He gripped the door-handle and put his shoulder against the door, ready to see if he could force it open, when, taking him by surprise, it swung open easily.

As he almost fell into the hall, Douglas emerged from the sitting room, looking his usual relaxed and friendly self, though slightly surprised.

"Sorry, I was just coming to let you in," he said. "Frances isn't quite herself, I'm afraid."

From behind him she screamed, "Be careful, he's got a gun!"

So it was not Frances who had been shot. Yet when she appeared in the doorway of her sitting room, she was staggering and there was blood down the front of her crumpled cotton dress and on her hands.

"He shot my two poor ducky darlings!" she shrieked. "They hadn't hurt him. They were only snarling. He shot them in cold blood. Oh, he's wicked, wicked!"

Douglas showed his teeth in a wide smile. He brought forward the hand that he had been holding behind his back. It held a gun in it in a casual fashion.

"The two damned creatures went for me, I don't know why," he said equably. "Stinking bloody brutes. They ought to have been put down years ago."

"It's a lie!" Frances cried. "They were faithful and intelligent. They were only showing you that if you hurt me they'd tear you to pieces. They would have too. I trusted them utterly."

It struck Catherine then that the smell of dog was far less strong in the house than it usually was. Frances had had the doors and the windows of the bungalow open all day and the dogs had been allowed to spend most of it in the garden. There was an unfamiliar smell of furniture polish besides, and the pungent scent of some detergent issuing from the kitchen.

"Well, come in, if corpses don't worry you," Douglas said. "Perhaps we might bury them presently. What brings you, by the way?"

He stepped aside to let Brian and Catherine into the house, then closed the door behind them.

"*I* brought them," Frances said. "You thought you had me here alone at your mercy, but I was able to summon friends. I have friends who understand me. Now, if you want to do any more murder, you'll find it difficult to explain away so many bodies."

"There she goes, talking of murder again," Douglas said with a kind of exasperation. "She rings me up and says she has something important to say to me, and I come at once and she starts accusing me of murder."

"Not till I saw your gun," Frances said. "What did you bring it for if you didn't think you might have to silence me?"

"I've been carrying this gun ever since I came back from the hospital," Douglas said. "It's an old friend. I've had it for years. You see, if someone wants me out of the way, I don't mean to make it too easy for them." He turned to Brian. "Don't believe what the old girl's told you. I didn't shoot them in cold blood at all. I stupidly took the gun out of my pocket, just to show her that I intended to defend myself next time, and she panicked and set the goddamned animals on me. Shooting them seemed the easiest way of defending myself."

"It's a lie," Frances said. "Every word is a lie."

"Frances, what *do* you know?" Brian asked with anxiety in his voice. "Why has Douglas suddenly become afraid of you?"

She sighed. "It's just that I know he's wicked, you see. He's very wicked. That's really all. But that's enough, isn't it?"

"And I thought she was fond of me," Douglas said with a laugh.

"I'm very fond of you, dearie, very fond indeed," she said. "That's why I wanted to talk to you, even though I believe you're capable of anything. When I think of those paintings of yours that I never hang up because they're so frightening, the ones with red paint all over them, like smears of blood . . . Oh yes, you're capable of anything. You always were. But I thought perhaps if we could have a sensible talk I could stop you going from bad to worse."

"Listen to her," Douglas said. "How long is it since she's been capable of talking sensibly?"

Brian went forward and gently thrust Frances aside from the sitting room doorway. Catherine followed him into the room. Frances seemed to want to prevent it and began to sob as they went in with dry, harsh, tearless sobs that shook her sagging body.

Catherine caught her breath at what she saw. She was not squeamish. Helping her father, she had seen blood, broken bones and torn flesh and had taught herself not to shrink from them. But the utter senselessness of the death of the two old fat dogs, lying there with blood still trickling out of the holes blasted into them on to Frances's recently vacuumed carpet, made her want to be sick.

Somehow it made it worse that the room was neat and clean. Frances's day of labour had resulted in the disappearance of all the fluff and cobwebs, there were no chewed bones in sight and the mahogany of the three pianos shone with polish. Even the jungle green of the walls looked less likely than usual to harbour snakes and dangerous insects.

Brian stood looking down at the dogs.

"Perhaps we ought to get on and bury them," he said. "The job'll be too much for Frances. Do you know where you want them put, Frances?"

"I don't know," she said. "I haven't thought. Under the apple trees at the top of the garden, perhaps. It doesn't matter."

All of a sudden she reached for one of the pictures that Douglas had painted and given to her when he had been a boy. With a gesture of astonishing force she smashed it across her knee. The frame shattered, the glass fell in fragments on the floor and she began to tear the painting into small pieces.

"That's no loss," Douglas said good-naturedly, "if it makes you feel better."

"Oh, you're wicked," she said. "You always have been. I knew it when you were a boy, though it didn't make me love you less. Having so many talents and never working at using any of them, I knew how that would twist you. I knew that you were doomed. But perhaps I even loved you more because of it. I thought, here was someone I could help. Because I'm very wicked too, you know. That's what so many people don't understand. I'm full of hate and envy and destructiveness. But I learnt, you see, you can live with those things inside you and not do anything to harm anyone. When it all gets too much for you and things begin to churn around inside you and you begin to feel afraid of what you may do, you can grab a paint-pot and start to paint something. Or start hammering it all out on the piano. Or if things have got really bad, you can get out the vacuum cleaner and drive it up and down and round and round and you can sing till you feel at peace again. I got you down here to explain all that to you. I saw your face when you heard about the bomb in the car, the terrible anger in it, and I felt afraid for you. So I wanted to explain to you that even if you've an enemy who's trying to kill you, you mustn't take revenge yourself. You must simply find a way of letting out your anger and fear in a way that won't destroy you."

"And that's all you wanted to say to me?" Douglas said in a dazed tone. "You just wanted to give me a lecture on original sin?"

"Naturally. It's so very important."

"So you needn't have brought your gun," Brian said. "But of course you thought she'd understood about Andie's murder and the bomb that was meant for Elspeth. No wonder you looked a bit vengeful when you found that hadn't worked."

Douglas turned to him, looking thoughtful.

"Can you explain what you mean?"

"I was just starting to tell Catherine about it when we

heard Frances's summons," Brian said. "I told Catherine, work it out backwards. Who would have been killed by that bomb if it hadn't happened that the weather was so fine? You drove the Rolls out into the drive, didn't you, and left it there and took off for London in the Lotus? And you left the keys in the Rolls, which you know Elspeth adores driving. So you could be fairly certain she'd go off in it some time during the day. And as soon as she opened the door, the whole thing would have gone off with a bang and she'd have been blown to pieces. But it just happened she had an emergency call from Frances that morning for help with picking her strawberries, and that's what she did all day. It was just the strawberries that saved her."

"Go on, go on," Douglas said. "That can't be all you've got to say."

"It's a good deal."

"And it's a good theory, of course. But you haven't mentioned, had I any motive for this action?"

"She'd had one try at killing you, hadn't she?" Brian said. "You must have thought she was likely to try it again. And I must say, I think you were right, and Irene thinks so too. That's why she's decided to take Elspeth away with her. It's a pity she didn't think of it sooner. All the same, sooner or later, Elspeth would be able to come back, and you'd never know for sure when you'd be safe from her."

"But this is news to me, that it was Elspeth who tried to kill me on Friday," Douglas said. "Has she confessed? Because I, of course, don't remember a single thing about it."

Brian shook his head. "I'm afraid I've never really believed in that amnesia of yours. If you ever really forgot anything, the memory came back pretty quickly. But you decided not to admit it, because if no one knew you'd remembered her attack on you, you'd appear to have no motive for harming her. All the same, I think you saw her approach with that branch she'd left ready to hit you with when a good moment came, and you remember how you were just too slow to save yourself and went down into the water."

"And then Andie saved me," Douglas said. "Are you forgetting that when you accuse me of murdering him? Andie saved my life."

"Andie saved the source of his income. Does a blackmailer need anyone quite as much as he needs his victim? But the victim can get on very nicely without the blackmailer."

"So you think Andie was a blackmailer?"

"Obviously. He knew all about the murder of June Hunnicut in Australia. He had those ear-rings. He may have taken them off the body himself. He may have known where it was buried. Perhaps he even helped you to bury her. I might have thought it was all the other way round if he hadn't so plainly got you in his power. Didn't you give him a house to live in? Didn't you buy some work of his whenever he was short of money? He doesn't seem to have been greedy as blackmailers go. Perhaps you wouldn't have worried too much about the small drain he was on you if that had been all. But he was a moody devil and he might have given you away one day out of sheer irresponsibility. As with Elspeth, you couldn't feel safe while he was around. So with Catherine as a witness, you worked on his jealousy so that his getting drunk and violent and at last murderous shouldn't seem too strange, and you knocked him out in the lodge and carried him up to the pool and dumped him in it. Then you forged that suicide note and I suppose spent the rest of the night manufacturing the bomb that was to look as if it was meant for you, but in fact was going to kill Elspeth. You were trying to kill two birds with one stone."

"Well," Douglas said slowly, "perhaps there isn't much point in arguing. It isn't really important, because, you see, I've got the gun. I can kill all three of you and take my chance, disappearing. You might not be found for two or three days, so I'd have a good start. Or I could hold you as hostages—your lives in exchange for a safe passage back to Australia. That's a good place to disappear in."

"I shouldn't try that, Douglas. It hardly ever works."

Douglas smiled. That he looked as good-natured as ever somehow made the moment worse.

"I suppose what you want, Brian, is to hand me over to the police and tell them this yarn of yours."

"It certainly seems the best thing to do."

"Without sparing a passing thought for the fact that Andie was a blackmailer and that Elspeth, that charming young girl, tried to drown me?"

"I'm sure allowance would be made for that at your trial."

"But am I so very much worse than either of them?"

"*What about my wife?*"

No one had heard Walter Hunnicut come into the bungalow. But he was in the doorway of the sitting room, crouching slightly, his weight on the balls of his feet. His hands hung loosely at his sides. His bronzed face had a greyish tinge and his eyes looked feverish.

"Was *she* a blackmailer? Did *she* try to kill you?" he demanded almost in a whisper.

The gun steadied in Douglas's hand.

"This is bad luck for you," he said. "You needn't have got mixed up in this. What brought you in?"

"I heard some shooting," the small man said. "And I've

heard a good deal more than that since I came in." He took a step forward. *"What about my wife?"*

"If you want to know, before I put a bullet into you," Douglas said, "she was a bloody nuisance. She'd set her heart on coming to England with me. Wouldn't listen to reason when I told her to go back to you. So I lost patience with her and broke her neck. I was sorry about it. I didn't mean to do it. But there's just so much you can stand, then you're apt to decide it's time to protect your own interests—"

A noise that Catherine had never heard come from a human throat before came deep out of the thin throat of Walter Hunnicut as he hurled himself at Douglas.

Douglas's finger tightened on the trigger.

Brian saw that tiny movement and threw himself at Douglas. But Frances was somehow between them. The gun wavered and the sound of the shot, deafening in the room, was followed by a wild scream.

Then Walter Hunnicut was upon Douglas with his hands on his throat and Douglas went down. The two rolled together on the carpet, stained by the dogs' blood, with blood smearing their clothes and their faces. Douglas was far the stronger of the two men, yet there was some weakness in the way he fought, as if he did not care what happened to him, perhaps even wanted to be defeated and have his brains beaten out.

It was Brian who prevented that, forcing a way between the two struggling men. He had hold of the gun by then.

"God, look at that!" Walter Hunnicut cried as he staggered to his feet.

He pointed.

In a heap on top of her dogs Frances lay quite still, with fresh blood on her face and her breast. Whether it was her own or that of her dogs, there was no telling.

CHAPTER THIRTEEN

"She'll live," Brian said, smiling as he joined Catherine and Superintendent Chase in the corridor outside the ward in the Paxley-Parton Hospital, to which Frances had been taken. "She's still unconscious, but it's mostly shock. That shot just grazed her scalp before it went into the dog. But she got a nasty knock on the head too when she fell. She's a tough one, though. She'll be out in a few days."

"She saved Hunnicut's life, to go by what you've told me," Mr. Chase said.

"He realises it," Brian said. "He's already sent her flowers. Armfuls of them. I don't know where he got them at this time of night."

"From Mr. Cookham," Catherine said. "That's to say, from my garden. He told me so. The two of them were out in the rain, picking flowers by torchlight and making them up into nice bunches for half an hour after the ambulance took Frances away."

"She was lucky," Mr. Chase said. "You know, I'd an idea she knew more than was healthy for her. It was something to do wih the way she guessed there was a bomb in the car and stopped Cable getting into it."

"I don't believe she knew anything definite," Brian said. "She's just got her own strange kind of insight."

"I suppose if Frances hadn't stopped Douglas getting

into the car," Catherine said, "he'd have found some other reason for not opening the door."

"You know, I can't help feeling she may have been trying to help him, giving him that reason," Mr. Chase said. "I believe myself she may have known more all along than she'll ever tell us. A very complex old lady, with a very sharp mind, even if she isn't what most of us think of as altogether normal. She's a kind of person, I'll admit, who scares me a little. The kind of person who is almost, but not quite, the same as the rest of us. I believe they scare me more than the really crazy ones. They've got a kind of power in them which they use in ways that'd never enter your mind. Even after all the experience I've had, they still give me gooseflesh. Well, I'll be off home." He yawned. "I could do with a quiet night. I've had a lot of different things on my mind recently."

"Yes, I suppose this case has been only one of your troubles," Brian said. "What will happen to Cable now? Have you enough solid evidence against him for a conviction?"

"We've got plenty from the way he's talking," Mr. Chase said. "The question is whether we'll keep him here or send him back to Australia, where he's wanted for the murder of that girl. He's confessed it and told us where he buried the body, with Manson's help. In any case, he'll get life. Good night now. See you at the inquest."

He strode off down the corridor.

"'With Manson's help . . .'" Catherine echoed him sadly. "Brian, I mean to keep my little carving. I may put it away out of sight, but I'm going to keep it. Because it was Andie threatening Douglas that he might tell me about June Hunnicut that made Douglas decide to kill him, wasn't it? That was the meaning of the quarrel they had that puzzled me so. Andie was ready to take a risk, trying to do his best for me."

A nurse was walking towards them down the long corridor. In spite of her, Brian put his arms round Catherine and kissed her on the mouth.

The nurse gave a singularly happy smile at the ceiling as she passed them, as if she somehow had a share in the moment.

3-2012